I0736198

MISTAKEN *Obsession*

EVE GRAFTON

Copyright @2020 by Eve Grafton

This publication contains the opinions and ideas of its author. It is intended to provide helpful and informative material on the subjects addressed in the publication. The author and publisher specifically disclaim all responsibility for any liability, loss or risk, personal or otherwise, which is incurred as a consequence, directly or indirectly, of the use and application of any of the contents of this book.

WORKBOOK PRESS LLC
187 E Warm Springs Rd,
Suite B285, Las Vegas, NV 89119, USA

Website: https://workbookpress.com/
Hotline: 1-888-818-4856
Email: admin@workbookpress.com

Ordering Information:
Quantity sales. Special discounts are available on quantity purchases by corporations, associations, and others. For details, contact the publisher at the address above.

Library of Congress
Control Number: 2016906460

ISBN-13:   978-1-952754-05-0 (Paperback Version)
                                    978-1-952754-06-7 (Digital Version)

REV. DATE: 03 / 12 / 2020

Chapter 1

Alessandro Rodrigos, manager of the Aria Hotel in Buenos Aires, stood at the barrier in the arrival hall of the international airport, holding up a placard reading 'Ms Bethany Randford'.

As the passengers of the aircraft that had just landed headed towards the immigration hall counters, his eyes alighted on a slim, young woman holding the hand of a small girl.

Thinking how delightful the young couple were, the young woman dressed in a dress of white daisies on a yellow background and high-heeled sandals, her long wavy hair held back by a yellow ribbon, she looked like a strip of sunshine on a foggy day amongst all the other tired and crumpled passengers, and the little girl skipped alongside of her, holding her hand, chattering away to the woman. He gazed at them until they disappeared behind a barrier.

He sighed, and looked around for the figure he was meeting, possibly a middle-aged woman, hair held back in a bun, wearing a crumpled suit, and she would be wearing horn-rimmed glasses and low-heeled shoes. As he gazed around, he heard a soft voice, saying, 'Hello, señor, I am Bethany Randford,'

Standing before him was the beautiful young woman that had caught his attention a few minutes earlier! His delight must have lit up his face, for Bethany laughed and said, 'You look surprised, señor.'

He felt himself blushing and replied, 'I was expecting a much older person', and laughed with her.

He took her luggage trolley, saying, 'Welcome to Argentina, Señorita Randford. I am Alessandro Rodrigos, manager of the Aria Hotel. The owner of the hotel, Señor Ortega, has bidden me to welcome you and offer to you any services required during your stay with us.'

'Call me Bethany', she said, 'and thank you.'
'And my friends call me Sandro. I hope you will be my friend.'
Bethany looked up at his tall figure and twinkling brown eyes and dark hair and decided that he was very handsome. 'Sandro it is then. I am so pleased that you speak English. I was afraid that I would have to use my phrase book to translate for me.'

As they loaded her luggage into the back of a dark-coloured SUV, Sandro asked if she wanted the tourist drive around Buenos Aires or go straight to the hotel.

'To the hotel, please. It is a twenty-six-hour journey from Perth in Western Australia to Buenos Aires. I was able to get some sleep on the aircraft flight, but what I would like now is a shower, change of clothes and then go for a walk. I have been sitting so long that I need some exercise, then have a light meal, and about 8 p.m. local time I would like to go to bed. I have always found that the best way to beat jet lag. You wake up in local time and can get more done.'

'It will be growing dark soon, Bethany, while you do all you have to do before your walk. Walking at night can be dangerous, especially for a woman walking alone. May I invite you to my house for a light meal? I live close by, just about the length of walk you will need from the hotel. I live with my parents, but they would not be intrusive.'

'I have a black belt in karate', she smiled at him. 'Anyone trying to interfere with me would wish they had not tried, so you do not have to worry about me. But I like your idea. I would not like to get lost on my first day here, and it is a good chance to get to know each other and for me to describe my mission here without others listening in.'

'As I said before, the owner of the hotel has asked me to look after you and go along with anything you want, so I am at your service. I will take you to your room, and when you are ready, just buzz the reception desk and they will find me. Would an hour be all right to do everything you need?'

'Just right', said Bethany, 'and thank you for your kind attention.'
'Well, here we are, the Hotel Aria. I will pick up your key, and the concierge will take your luggage to your room within minutes.'
'Is this a hotel car, Sandro?' she questioned.
'No, it belongs to me. The hotel hires cars to pick up clients. We find it cheaper than having our own cars and have to employ drivers for them. Also, the cars are smarter too than having one linger here, waiting to be used.'

They went to the second floor in the lift, and Sandro showed her into a modern room with en suite, not very big but adequate and very clean. She laid her handbag and computer on the desk as he explained, 'There is always an English-speaking person on the reception desk, although, of course, Spanish is our national language and used everywhere else. If you need a translator at any time, you can always call on me. I will see you in an hour, Bethany.'

After hanging up her clothes, promptly delivered by the concierge, she showered and changed into jeans and a cream-coloured silk shirt and low walking shoes, and the hour was up. She made her way to the reception desk and asked them to buzz Sandro, and he was there right away.

He took her arm and guided her through the foyer to the busy street. As they strolled, Sandro said cautiously, 'So you do not get embarrassed, I must explain that my father is in a wheelchair. He speaks quite good English. My mother, however, does not speak English. She only has Spanish and Italian. Her parents were immigrants here from Sicily in the 1960s.'

'Good', said Bethany. 'I speak Italian. My grandparents came from Italy about the same time, but they are from the north of Italy, as you can tell by my fair hair. My grandparents had a small farm in the countryside of Western Australia. My brother and I went to stay there almost every school holiday, and they would speak only Italian to us while we were there so that we would learn it. Does your father have an illness, Sandro?'

'No, he was shot by an employee at his ranch on the pampas. We have had a ranch forever that now belongs to my father and will someday be mine. It is passed down to the eldest son, so I will pass it down to my eldest son. We lived there for the first fourteen years of my life. We also have a town house. That is where we are going now. Many years ago my grandfather retired from the ranch to the town house, and we lived at the ranch, which we all loved.

'I have an older sister named Ana. My mother drove Ana to Buenos Aires every Monday to stay at our grandparents' house until Friday, so that she could attend school at a good girls' school. She picked her up again on Friday to bring her home for the weekend. I caught the local school bus to take me to the local town for school.

'We have a farm manager. His name is Matias, and his wife is Maria, and they had a twenty-two-year-old son called Miguel. They live in a cottage on the ranch, and Miguel was employed at the property as well. Miguel had got in with the wrong crowd in the town and would often come home late and very drunk, which meant that he had hangovers in the mornings and was surly and sometimes did not come to work at all, which annoyed my father very much, but he put up with it for Matias' sake because he is a long-time employee and a trusted friend.

'One Sunday, we had gone to church, leaving Ana home alone, as she had an exam next day at school and all the week also and wanted to study.

'When we arrived home, we could hear Ana screaming. Father jumped out of the car and ran up to Ana's room and found Miguel trying to rape her. Father was so angry, he grabbed Miguel and marched over to Matias' house and told them what Miguel had attempted to do, saying he had enough of Miguel and he was to leave the ranch by morning, and he did not want to see him back again. He would deliver Miguel's pay packet after dinner, and that would be the last of it.

'The next morning Mother took Ana to Buenos Aires and I caught the school bus as usual. Father went on his horse to check the water situation for the stock, usually Miguel's job. After doing that, he went to remount his horse, and as he climbed up, a shot rang out and the bullet hit him in the back. It was supposed to be a head shot to kill, but because he moved up, it caught him in the centre of the back. The horse was startled and ran back to the stables with the reins hanging. Matias heard the shot. He was working elsewhere on the property, but it is a sound common on the range, so he ignored it.

'Unable to move, my father lay there all day. I came home from school on the bus and saw my father's horse with the reins hanging and no sign of my father. I panicked and rang the emergency bell. Matias heard it and raced in from the range, and we both set off to search for Father. Matias knew the system of work and so we were able to find him quickly. Matias rang for an ambulance and the police. Each of us guessed what had happened. There was no sign of Miguel, but an empty cartridge shell from his gun was found in a grove of trees adjacent to where my father was found.

'Our lives changed that day! One day we were living our dream life and the next day everything changed. Because of my father's injury we moved to Buenos Aires to the town house. I had to change school. Money became an issue because of the hospital and medical bills, and my father was paralysed for life.' There was a silence for a moment. Then Bethany asked, 'Was Miguel caught?'

'No, he is loose somewhere. We will forever be looking over our shoulders in case he shows up. Matias stayed at the ranch as manager, and we return there at the property every second weekend to check on things and do what is needed.'

Bethany looked around as Sandro slowed and saw that they were in a nice housing area and stopping at the gate of a large property of brick and red tiles. Showing to the street were many windows with iron grilles and wooden shutters beside them, and in the centre was the biggest door she had ever seen in a private home. Sandro put a key in the lock and swung the door open for her to enter into a large courtyard with balconies on three sides and gaily coloured bougainvillea and sweet-smelling jasmine cascading from the balconies and earthenware pots on the ground.

Bethany gasped, 'It is magnificent! How wonderful!' Turning around, she saw a tall upright lady with dark hair in a bun at the nape of her neck, dressed beautifully in a multicoloured caftan. Next to her in a wheelchair was a man who looked so much like Sandro, it could only be his father.

Bethany moved to them and, speaking in Italian, introduced herself to Señora Rodrigos and turned to the man in the wheelchair, did the same in English, apologising because she had no Spanish. Sandro then excused them and moved to the opposite side of the courtyard and showed her into a colourfully decorated room to a dining table set with empanadas and salad, a decanter of wine, a jug of iced water, and a colourful bowl of fruit.

Bethany breathed, 'My, you certainly know how to spoil a girl!'
Sandro gave her a quizzical look. 'You like it, señorita?'
Bethany gave a giggle. 'Oh yes, I like it, señor! But I will not have the wine tonight, or I may not be able to walk back to the hotel. Iced water looks good right now, thank you.' As he poured the water, she asked, 'Tell me about the house. What is its history?'

They started the meal, and Sandro explained, 'My great-grandfather, or it may have been my great-great-grandfather, I am not too sure, had the houses built about 1905. There had been a gaucho disturbance, so he had the houses built for the family's safety and for a town house when they visited the city. My parents live in the left-hand side, my grandmother lives in the centre, and I live alone in this one. My grandfather died a year ago, so Grandmother has her freedom now, and you can find her most evenings at her bridge club.'

After they finished eating, Sandro said, 'Come I will show you around my unit. All of them have the same dimensions, but each generation who has lived here have had their own ideas about decorating, so it has turned out a bit eclectic. The rooms are big and airy and stay cool during the hot summers. In winter we have nice fires to keep us warm.'

Coming back to the main room, Bethany said, 'I have enjoyed your hospitality so much, Sandro, but I am so tired my head is ringing. I must get some sleep. I am sorry to leave because I have enjoyed your hospitality and your company so much. Before I go, I would like to thank your mother, as I suspect the supper was your mother's doing.'

Sandro laughed, 'Yes, she is a great cook, and her empanadas are the best you can get anywhere. She got the recipe from her sister in Chile. She also set the table for us.'

Señora Rodrigos answered her door and invited her in. Bethany thanked her in Italian for the meal and asked if she might return in two or three weeks', time, before she returned to Australia. She then turned to Señor Rodrigos and shook his hand and, in English, said, 'And you, señor, perhaps you can tell me some stories of the real Argentina. I look forward to your invitation. Goodbye for now.'
A broad smile came over his face, and he said, 'You will be very welcome, señorita. It has been our pleasure to meet you.'

As Sandro and Bethany walked from the house, he said, 'Thank you, Bethany, for being so gracious to my parents. My father does not get out too often, because it tires him.'

He turned to her. 'What an interviewer you make! You haven't yet revealed anything about yourself or your "mission here" as you call it.'

Bethany laughed. 'You have such an interesting history that it has not entered my mind about what I am doing here! And I am not easily distracted.'

She paused for a while before going on and said, 'You do know that your hotel is for sale?'

He nodded, and she went on, 'I am here because my company is interested, and I am here to see if it is worth the investment and to enquire of its future.

This means that I am going to have a fast course of the hotels around its area in the same range. The accountant back in Australia is checking the books and your señor Ortega has given me two weeks for a definite answer, for which I am very grateful, and it seems he has given me you, for which I am even more grateful. Both to him and especially to you, as your help will make everything much easier for me.'

'That seems a big responsibility for such a young person. What qualifications do you have for this job?'

'I have a degree in finance and business management from the university in Western Australia I attended, and I also have a diploma in hospitality, mainly in hotels. I have spent some time since graduating working for my father's company, checking hotels across Australia and Europe, although this is my first time in South America. I will be sending reports back to an accountant in Australia, but the decision is mine to make whether to purchase or not.

'Would you make an appointment for me to see Señor Ortega sometime next week, please? Is he well enough to see me, and does he speak English?'

'First of all, he does speak English. He has not been well. He was diagnosed with prostate cancer three years ago and handed over the management of the hotel to me. He did not have a son of his own and treated me as his son. I owe him all I know about the hotel and much more. He also taught me English and arranged for me to attend English lessons two nights a week to learn. His idea was that we would be having more people coming from the United States of America and from Europe, and most would speak some English, and he was right. A big percentage of clients are from those countries and Australia too.

'He has two daughters of his own, both married and living in the United States, who visit only occasionally and never come to the hotel. It is the daughters who want the hotel sold. They do not want to inherit a hotel. It is too much trouble for them. But the money would come in handy, they told their parents! Señora Ortega also wants the hotel sold to lift the worry from her husband, as his prognosis is not good. He is in his seventieth year. His mind is quite clear, but he knows he does not have very long, so an early decision would be welcomed.'

'Well,' said Bethany, 'with you to help me in the next week or whatever it needs, then he will have my decision. Under the circumstances, I am appreciative that he has given me time to decide.'

'Certainly I will help', said Sandro. 'What is it you want me to do?'
Bethany pulled out a written list from the pocket of her jeans and read out:

1.Visit as many boutique hotels in the area as possible in the time allowed.
2.If these hotels cater for meals, I would like to try them out for lunches.
3.Visit hotels that had entertainment with dinner and try them out.
4.See as much of Buenos Aires in between as possible.
5.Check politics and, of course, see around the Hotel Aria.

If you are able to come with me for all these things, your language skills will be invaluable, and I will pay all the expenses, including transport fuel and meals.

'My goodness,' exclaimed Sandro, 'you do have it worked out! I had no idea what this was all about. Señor Ortega merely said, "Give you all the help you need without saying why." I am delighted that you have included me in your timetable. It will be very instructive I can see. I don't know why I have not thought of it for myself. I have really just followed my boss' example. He is not a forward-thinking man, and to him his time-honoured traditions have worked well for him.

Things are changing. Since I have been manager, I have been able to modernise some of the rooms, such as the one you are staying in, but he would not change anything else. His father started the hotel many, many years ago, and before that, I believe, it had been a private house, but there is no sign of that now.'

Bethany asked, 'How did you come to be at the hotel, Sandro?'
'Señor Ortega took me on when I was a schoolboy looking for vacation work to help supplement the family income during their financial woes. He listened to me and started me straightaway on breakfast duties.

He taught me English and enrolled me in classes, and he has taught me everything I know, so I owe him a great deal.'

They had now entered the hotel reception area, and Sandro asked if she would like a wake-up call for the morning. If she ordered breakfast for nine o'clock, he could join her to discuss the first item on her list.

Bethany laughed and agreed that nine o'clock was fine for breakfast but not to worry about the wake-up call, as she had an alarm on her wristwatch and she may wake early and go for a walk to check out the location.

Sandro walked her to the door of her room and left, saying, 'Sleep well, señorita.'

Strangely, she felt a loss for a moment, but her bed looked too in viting to think of anything else.

Chapter 2

The following morning Bethany woke at seven o'clock, showered and dressed in the clothes she had worn the previous evening, and let herself out of the hotel and went for the walk she had promised herself, going this time in the opposite direction than they had gone last night.

She walked through the throng of people going to their day's work. She saw some small shops with people setting up a large restaurant on a corner and read the menu posted on a window and decided that it had to be added to her 'To do' list. A few dress shops, a men's store, all caught her eye for a future visit before going home to Australia, but she saw no department stores; they must be in a different part of town. She wended back towards the hotel via a long boulevard with a tramline down the centre and shady trees lining both sides of the street.

She checked her watch and had to sprint back to the hotel for her 9 a.m. appointment for breakfast.

She quickly had a wash, changed into a clean shirt, combed her hair and renewed her make-up, and went to meet the manager of the hotel for breakfast.

Sandro was seated at a table by the window and stood up when she entered.

As he gazed at her, he felt his heart give a lurch and felt confused. He then realised he was so happy to see her smiling at him. Whilst they helped themselves to the buffet, they discussed where they would go first.

They decided on a tour of the city highlights for the morning, followed by a lunch at a small hotel Bethany had found on the Internet, then back to the hotel and a rest for her, and some office work for him and meet back in the foyer at eight o'clock for dinner at the restaurant she had found on the corner of the street that morning during her walk.

Sandro drove the tourist trail, pointing out the university, some of the feature buildings, then to the football ground 'La Boca' that had been made famous by Maradona. They saw young couples busking on the pavements, doing the tango and added to the money collected in the hats laid out.

At lunch in the dining room of the small hotel they had chosen, Sandro remarked that last evening he had spoken to his parents. His father had suggested that Bethany go with them to the ranch this weekend. It would be Friday from four o'clock (so they arrived before dark) to Sunday, leaving the ranch at four o'clock to arrive back in the city before dark. It would show her a different side of life in Argentina.

Bethany instantly said, 'Oh yes, please! That sounds wonderful!' Then she thought about it for a minute and said, 'But I have never ridden a horse!'

Sandro laughed and said there were other means to getting around if she preferred it, but he would be happy to teach her to ride a horse. He would let his parents know she would be coming so they can cater for her.

The first day had turned out well, and the restaurant evening meal turned out to be a happy occasion. It was Bethany's first Argentine steak, a huge steak cooked just right, and a very tasty salad and a bottle of wine, accompanied by a guitar-playing singing waiter. It was a truly memorable evening, a fine festive meal, and she loved every minute of it, especially the time spent with Sandro with his easy manner; it was such a pleasure to be with him.

They walked back to the hotel hand in hand, and it felt so natural.

****

The next day was much the same – a boutique hotel with photos of Argentina lining the walls of the dining room, with a very nice meal and a glass of wine.

As they arrived back at the Aria Hotel, Sandro suggested that now was a good time to look through the hotel, as the day staff would have just left and it would be a short while before the evening staff came on.

The hotel was quiet as he showed her around the bedroom areas of those that were not occupied that day. Thirty had been modernised at the front of the building and new plumbing and lighting put in recently.

The remainder of the rooms were in original condition, although nicely decorated in an older style. Sandro explained that the price for the modernised rooms were double of the original ones. They had good turnover of the original rooms. Many of the patrons were salesmen or ranchers coming into town for a few days and brought their wives to shop, and not everyone could afford the higher prices. Many of them had been coming for years and preferred the cheaper rooms, even though they had to share the bathrooms. All the prices were room-only. If they wanted breakfast, they had to pay extra, and surprisingly, most didn't mind paying for their breakfast.

In the area that looked like a ballroom, Sandro explained that they used to have a restaurant here with entertainment, but the government had closed all nightclubs in 2004, because there had been a fire in one nightclub and many people had died. Even though the Hotel Aria was not a nightclub, they too were closed down.

Although the ban had been lifted sometime ago, Señor Ortega had not wanted to start it up again, so the room was unused, except for a few tables and a small bar to serve non-alcoholic drinks through the day.

The ballroom had a Spanish look to it, very high ceilings decorated in gilt and gilded decorative panels on the walls and gilded pillars at the doorway to the entrance. Bethany could almost see ladies in formal wear dancing to the sound of guitars. It was a beautiful room!

Another room was the 'Smokers room' – brown leather Chesterfield chairs and sofas and photos on the walls of gauchos on the pampas and horse-drawn carriages. Sandro explained that this room was generally used by the older men, including his father from time to time, to chat with his compatriots about days gone by. Someone always had a guitar, and the room could get raucous sometimes as they sang their songs and relived their youth.

The kitchen was outdated and would need remodelling if food was to be prepared from there.

Then there was the breakfast room, a long room that ran down the side of the ballroom but separated from it by a wall – used by all the clients from seven to ten each morning for a buffet breakfast.

The hotel was a mixture of old and new, and everything was spotlessly clean, so the staff was doing a good job.

Sandro introduced her to Daniel Sanchez, who was the assistant manager and had been promised extra wages to look after things while Sandro was busy with her this week, or two if necessary. Bethany congratulated them both on the appearance of the hotel; they had not known of the buyer's inspection, and everything was in very good order.

Bethany wrote up her report each afternoon, and so far the only negative found was the kitchen, which she felt could be fixed without too much trouble.

She wondered if she was seeing things through rose-coloured glasses, because of her growing infatuation with Sandro! She mentally shook herself. It had only been a few days! Don't be ridiculous! Though she looked forward to the evenings outing with him!

They were going to a well-known chain hotel/restaurant that evening to try out the high side of town, so it meant she would have to dress up a bit. She put on a slim black dress and wore high-heeled gold sandals and gold necklace and earrings, with her hair loose around her shoulders.

Sandro called for her at eight o'clock, and she went down to meet him. She stared at the sight of him dressed in a black suit and tie.

Looking so formal! Wow, he was so handsome! She felt her heart go ping. She had never had that feeling before in her life!

He in turn looked stunned at her and murmured into her ear as he took her arm, 'I like it, señorita. You are very beautiful!'

And he escorted her to the chauffer-driven car that would be taking them to their location and picking them up again at eleven o'clock.

The hotel was very shiny and smart with very high ceilings, and the restaurant was smart too, with lanterns on each table and low overhead lighting, which made the seating intimate. Bethany felt quite relaxed in the intimate atmosphere with Sandro for company. He appeared to blend into any background and had been greeted by the maitre d' as if he was well known.

After the main course, there was an exhibition of tango danced to a background of piano accordion and guitars. Bethany loved the show. She had seen tango exhibitions at home and had always loved the art, but in this beautiful room with Sandro beside her, it seemed especially special, and she was spellbound. She felt Sandro move and take her hand. She turned and looked at him to see him with a slight smile looking at her. She had never felt so content in her life.

Eleven p.m. came too soon and broke the mood and brought her down to earth. She had been in a dream, which must end soon. She would be going home!

Sandro courteously showed her to the door of her room and spoke quietly, 'Goodnight, Bethany. Sweet dreams. I will see you at nine o'clock for breakfast', and turned away to the stairs.

She stood inside her door and could feel her heart pumping. She had enjoyed the evening, so much, she had not wanted it to end.

Chapter 3

At breakfast next morning Bethany asked Sandro if he would take her to the Plaza de Mayo, where the mothers of the disappeared during Argentina's 'dirty war' had demonstrated.

A still look came over his face, and he asked, 'Do you know this story all the way over in Australia?'

'Yes, it is a well-known story in the history of Argentina. When the facts came out to the world, everyone was aghast that a government could do such horrible things to their own citizens.'

Sandro was quiet for a moment. 'My uncle was one of the disappeared, my father's older brother. He was living in the town house with his grandparents whilst he was attending university and became entwined in the politics on campus, and one day he just did not come home. We still do not know what happened to him. My uncle was five years older than my father and presumably would have taken over the ranch in time, but it went to my father as next in line.

'It was a very sad period of time for many families, something we will never allow to happen again. Yes, I will take you to the Plaza de Mayo.'

'I am so sorry, Sandro.' She paused and then went on, 'The child whose hand I was holding at the airport – her name is Elle – is coming to meet her great-grandmother who is one of the madres. Her eldest son and daughter-in-law and their six-month-old baby girl disappeared.

'There was so much trouble for the family at the time that they sent their younger son out of Argentina. I do not know how he managed it, but he was accepted as an immigrant into Australia. He grew up, married an Australian girl, and had a daughter, Elena, who is now married and has two children. This story has always made me sad. Elena has been my friend since schooldays, so when I knew I was coming here to Buenos Aires, I paid her fares for her to come with me so she could meet her grandmother. Also, I must confess, to be my translator, if I needed one I could trust. However, I did not know that Señor Ortega would provide me with a translator I can trust and I must tell him how much I appreciate you.'

Sandro reached for her hand. 'Thank you, señorita. I have made an appointment for you to see Señor Ortega on Tuesday. So, we have the ranch to visit this weekend and you will have time to recover from the horse riding {this with a wicked grin} before meeting him. However, do you mind if we go to the Plaza de Mayo on Monday? I have quite a lot of work to catch up on here at the hotel today. Shall we go to another boutique hotel tonight for dinner, one with entertainment?'

'How well you understand me, señor!' breathed Bethany. 'I shall go to the city today and meander around the shops. I will ring Elena to come with me, so if I have trouble with the language, she can help me out. We will have lunch in the city, and I will see you tonight at eight o'clock.'

'I will look forward to it', Sandro said. 'Happy shopping!'

****

Bethany rang Elena, and they made a time and a place. Then she asked the reception to order her a taxi.

Elena was on time, and they wandered around looking into shops and then stopped at a small cafe for coffee and a snack.

Bethany quizzed Elena on her reception from her grandmother.

Elena gave a broad smile. 'It is amazing how well preserved she is in mind and spirit, considering all the sorrows in her life, losing both sons, and sadly her husband died two years ago. She is so happy to have this time with us, to be with the children. She has lost a whole generation of her family. The children loved her straightaway. You know how Elle can chatter? Well, now you would think Spanish was her first language. They waved goodbye to me today with no worries about her leaving them with the old lady.'

Bethany asked if there were any disturbances in Argentina, seeing as the past had been quite disturbed at times. She said she felt a little distant from the general population by her lack of Spanish.

Elena thought for a minute. 'I have not got out much myself because of the children, but from what the old ladies who visited her grandmother said, there is quite a lot of poverty. There was a distinct rich side, a middle side and a poor side, even a squalid side. I guess, like many big cities.

'Wages were very low, and many struggled to make ends meet, but life went on. There is a violent side too, so it is best not to go out alone at night, although it seems daytime is not a problem.

'The general population seemed now to think they have the right to demonstrate, and at any time of day you can hear the sounds of drums or saucepans clanging as people gathered to march about something or other. There was no sign of the past disturbances, though these demonstrations seem to be quite fun.

'A faint hope for the moment for Grandmother is that DNA is finding many of the children that disappeared with their parents all that time ago. It seems many of the children were taken from their parents by the politicos and army officials, and some of these children have now come forward to be tested. Grandmother has hoped that her grandchild will come forward to be reunited with her.'

Bethany shuddered. It was terrible story. How hard it must have been for Elena's family to have gone through all that!

'Thank you, Bethany, for making this trip possible for me, and especially for Grandmother!'

They wandered around looking at store windows for a while, and it struck Bethany how well everyone was so well dressed. 'Everybody is much more casual at home', she commented.

Bethany bought a toy for each of Elena's children, and they went their own way back to children and hotel.

She was tired when she arrived back at the hotel, so much activity and so many late nights, so she lay down on her bed and went off to sleep. When she awoke, she was startled to see that it was 7.30 p.m. She rang the reception and asked whether Sandro had been enquiring after her. The girl there said she did not expect Sandro until eight o'clock because he had to help his father to bed every evening.

The penny dropped for Bethany. Of course, how thoughtless of her not to realise why it was nine in the morning and eight each evening! Because he had to help his father! How selfish she had been not to think of it for herself!

She hastily showered and changed. This would be the last hotel outing, as they were going to the ranch the nest day for the weekend.

The hotel they went to was in a tree-lined street and attractive from the outside. Inside there were artefacts and ornaments lining the passageway and a tiny shop selling postcards and woollen handmade ponchos. Bethany bought some postcards to send back home to her family and friends.

The meal was light and tasty and the wine fruity. The entertainment started with a tango and ended with flamenco with guitars strumming in the background. It was received very well by the diners, including Sandro and Bethany. It was similar to the show they had seen the previous evening but more casual. The restaurant was not large, and all the seats were taken and seemed to be a popular place.

After the entertainment, they had their dessert, and she asked Sandro about the ranch and said she would like to take his parents a gift and whether he could recommend something.

He thought for a moment and suggested one of the ponchos in the gift shop where she had purchased the postcards. It could get very cold in winter on the pampas, and the poncho was easy to wear, whether riding a horse or shopping.

When they were leaving, Sandro asked the receptionist to open the shop for them to make a choice. Bethany chose a lovely mauve with a touch of orange in the borders for Señora Rodrigos, and asked Sandro to choose one for his father. He chose a heavier wool in green, just the right length for someone in a wheelchair or on a horse.

She paid with her credit card, and they were gift-wrapped separately, as they were too big for one package. She thought they were much nicer than she had seen that day in the city shops, so she felt very happy with her purchases.

Chapter 4

After breakfast next morning Bethany washed her hair, washed some clothes, did some ironing, and packed a small bag ready for the weekend ahead and then went for a walk.

This time was a different direction again. She felt she was starting to know her way around. Everywhere it was busy with shoppers and tourists. As she wandered, she noticed that there were statues down almost every avenue. It was a very attractive city and well kept.

As she returned to the hotel, she suddenly knew Sandro was behind her. She turned, and there he was. How extraordinary that she had felt the electricity between them! He held out his hand. She took it, and he drew her into his office without saying a word. They stood close for a moment. Then he moved to his desk and said casually, 'Are you ready to leave now, Bethany? We like to leave early to arrive before dark. It is two hours' drive.'

Bethany came out of her spell. 'All packed and ready to go. Do not forget to take the gifts', gesturing to the parcels by the door. 'I will just run up and get my bag.'

The SUV was standing at the entry when she returned, and Sandro took her bag from her and placed it into the back of the vehicle, along with the gift parcels. 'Is that all you need?' he asked.

'Yep, I like to travel light', she answered.
He led her to the front passenger side of the vehicle and explained that his father would be sitting here during the trip, as it was too hard to get him into and out of the back seat. 'As I will be driving, you will sit in the back with my mother.'

At the house, Señora Rodrigos welcomed them in with coffee and cake before the journey. Bethany felt quite at home with them and said she loved the cake served with the coffee. Señora Rodrigos said in Italian, 'I love that I can talk to you in Italian. Where did you learn it?'

'From my grandparents, my mother's parents. They were immigrants to Australia about the same time you came to Argentina. They purchased a small farm in the south of Western Australia growing mostly fruit. They had a cow for milk and a few chickens and a few sheep.

My brother and I stayed almost every school holiday with them, and my grandparents would only speak Italian to us so that we would learn it. It is an old friend now.'

While Sandro loaded things into the vehicle and helped his father into the front passenger seat, Bethany helped clear the table and wiped the dishes.

The trip was interesting, and she was amazed how flat the countryside was away from the city. They passed through small towns, past farms or estancias as they were called here, and came to a pair of tall gates, which Sandro opened with a remote control. The gates lent a majesty to the ranch house she could see. They drove up a wide driveway to a beautiful house set among shrubs and trees and parked in the garage connected to the house.

Bethany and the señora carried in the smaller packages and luggage, leaving Sandro to carry the bigger bags and help his father into the wheelchair. The entrance to the house from the garage opened directly into the kitchen, which was huge in Bethany's estimation, about twice the size of her kitchen at home. It was old-fashioned by today's standards but was obviously efficient and able to cater for a large crowd. The room felt very homely and comfortable. There were quarry tiles on the floors, through the main rooms with rugs colourfully positioned, and up to the stairs to the bedrooms. All the rooms had a homely feeling and were quite big.

Sandro took Bethany's bag in one hand and her hand in his other and took her upstairs to the room she would be using during her stay.

'This was my sister Ana's room when we lived here, but she has not been back to it for a long time. The bathroom is just down the passage. Come down to supper when you are ready.'

A cosy atmosphere in the kitchen/dining room instead of the formal dining room put Bethany at ease, and she helped the señora heat a pot of soup and cut some crusty bread and made a salad from the food basket brought in from the car, whilst the señora cut some ham and placed a bowl of fruit on the table and prepared some coffee for after the meal. It was all done quickly, and the señora clapped her hands when they had finished, saying, 'Thank you, Bethany. I usually do these things alone. It is good to have help.'

The men came into the room when she called to them, and Sandro pulled out her chair for her to sit down. The talk was easy whilst they were eating, and after the meal, Sandro excused them to Bethany and wheeled his father out to a bedroom on the ground floor.

He explained that it had formerly been the quarters for the housekeeper, but had been renovated for his parents. There was a bedroom, bathroom, and lounge room. The señora also excused herself and went to help her husband.

Bethany cleared the table and washed the dishes and then wandered around. She looked at the books in the bookshelves, but they were in Spanish, of course!

She sat down on the sofa before the unlit fireplace and dozed off until Sandro returned, apologising for leaving her alone so long.

'Come, Bethany, I will show you around the garden or as much as we can see in the growing darkness. Tomorrow I will take you for a drive around the property and introduce you to Matias and Maria, but earlier than that, I must help my father do a few chores around the place that are necessary. So have a sleep in and then help yourself to breakfast when you are ready, and I will be back at about ten o'clock for coffee.'

They strolled in the garden at the rear of the house where grapevines grew over the pergola and fruit trees shone silver in the fading light. The stables were a short distance from the house, and Sandro introduced the horses to her. The first three were quite big and then they came to a smaller bay mare.

'This is Betsy and will be your horse. She is very quiet and will not buck you off', he said, giving her a wicked grin again as he said it.

'I hope you are teasing me, Sandro. I am usually game to try anything, and Betsy looks docile to me – well, at the moment anyway.'

The sky was darkening, and they sat under the pergola and watched the stars come out and the moon come up. They were all so clear you felt you could reach up and touch the stars. The perfume of the trees and the hay from the stables travelled to them; it was so heady there must be jasmine nearby too. It was so lovely that Bethany felt as if she should pinch herself to make sure she was awake and not dreaming!

A week ago she had been sitting alone at home flicking through a hotel magazine when she saw the advertisement of the sale of a hotel, and now she was here with a handsome courteous man in this paradise, totally at ease with him as if she had known him for years. At this moment she did not want to go home!

Sandro said, 'Come, my lovely. I can see you are tired. It has been a long day.' Sandro's room was next to hers on the upstairs landing, and he took her hand to climb the stairs. Neither felt like leaving the other, but nothing was said, and they went to their own rooms.

****

Bethany heard Sandro going down the stairs at 5 a.m. but snuggled back to sleep. When she awoke later, she looked around the room that had been Ana's. There were floral curtains at the large window and green carpet to tone in. The furniture was antique, but the room was big enough to take the wardrobes, dressing table, carved headboard to the bed, and matching carving on an easy chair and on the wardrobes. It was a beautiful room for a young girl growing up.

She looked out of the window and could see Sandro and his father on horseback talking to another man, who must be Matias. Señor Rodrigos seemed to have a special saddle to hold him on the horse.

'So for a new adventure', she thought as she showered and dressed in jeans and T-shirt and low-heeled shoes. The she tied her hair back into a ponytail with just a few curls around her face. She grabbed a hat and went downstairs to the kitchen.

The señora was in the kitchen and greeted her happily. She was baking scones for the morning coffee, but offered to cook something for her guest. 'No, thank you. I just have coffee and toast and a piece of fruit, but I can see the scones are nearly ready, so I will wait for them instead of toast.'

The señora asked if she lived with her parents.

'No, señora, my mother died when I was sixteen, and my mother's parents came to live with my father, my brother, and myself when their daughter died. They stayed with us until my brother and I had finished school and university.

'They then moved into a retirement village. I bought a town house for myself. My brother got married, and my father was alone for some time and then met and married a lovely lady three years ago, and they have a new son.

I live alone because of my job. I do a lot of travelling, so it is easier for everyone that I have my own house. I am quite happy to be by myself.'

She heard a movement at the door and turned to see Sandro standing there. He asked with a grin, 'No sweethearts to keep you company?'

'I haven't had time to cultivate a relationship. I always seem too busy. I do have friends, mostly from my university days, but we usually go out in a group, and that is fine for me. Are we ready to go for our ride now?'

He laughed and said, 'After I have had my coffee, and perhaps it would be more comfortable in the car as there is quite a distance around the borders, we will check the fences as we drive. We will save Betsy for later to ride out and see the sunset in the cool of the evening.'

While they were riding, Bethany remarked, 'I admire your management skills, Sandro. Whether it is at the hotel or here at the ranch, you are very much in charge. How do you see your future? Do you want to stay on at the hotel if it is sold?'

'I love "my" hotel', he said. 'I have been there half my life. However, the new management may see it differently and prefer to have an older person in charge. In that case, there is always the ranch to fall back on. I could increase the stock. We have cut back on the cattle we used to run because we have only one aging man to take care of the property, but we have room to run more cattle if I were to live here permanently.

My father's medical bills are not such a problem, as they have been in the past, so we do not need so much to keep us going.

'I cannot see myself going to another hotel and starting at the bottom, after being in charge for so long.

'I loved the ranch as a boy. Growing up here was wonderful. I missed it badly when we moved to the city, and I think I could be happy living here again.'

Bethany grinned, 'No sweetheart to keep you company?'
His head swung around to her, and he said seriously, 'Not yet, señorita, but I have hope!'

That silenced Bethany for a while.
As they worked their way back towards the house, Bethany asked, 'What happened to Ana? Nobody mentions her.'

Sandro glanced at her for a second and explained, 'Ana finished her schooling and was asked at a party if she would model for reputable modelling company in the city, which has international connections. Our father was not too happy about it, but could not come up with a real excuse to stop her. She worked in the major store in the city and was very successful. She had many invitations from men but generally turned them down. I don't think she realised her effect on the male population. I thought she turned them down because of the situation at home.

'My father had a male nurse for the first two years of his paraplegia. This chap was named Frank, something or other, who lived in the unit I live in now because he was on call mostly mornings and evenings, seven days a week. What no one realised for some time was the fascination Frank had for Ana. He was a muscular fellow, quite good-looking, about twenty-seven years old, I think. One evening Father could not get off to sleep. He heard Ana leaving our house and going to Frank's house. She did not come back till 5 a.m.

'Father was so angry and called in Frank and Ana for a showdown. The outcome was that Frank was dismissed and Ana moved out of the house to a flat that she shared with other girls, until she was twenty-one and then moved overseas on a contract for the modelling agency.

'I became the nurse. I was sixteen at the time. I spent most of my time between the hotel, the school, and the house. Father refused to have another nurse or a "stranger in the house" ever again.

'At that time, my parents were coming to the ranch each weekend, and Matias helped my father into bed and on his horse, but it was getting too much for Matias.

'My mother used to drive the car, but Father was critical of her driving, and she got nervous. So, that became my job as well, as I had recently got my driver's license, but because of my shifts at the hotel, we had to make it fortnightly.

'We have not seen Ana since she left Argentina. She stayed in France, modelling, until she married a doctor and gave up her work to have two children. As far as I know, she has never returned to Argentina. She writes to me on my birthday, though, and sends photos of her children. The eldest is a girl and very much like her. The boy is a real Rodrigos. He looks uncannily like Father and me. Quite spooky really!'

They were nearing a grove of trees and a water tank and a clearing, and Sandro pointed out to her the spot where his father had been shot by Miguel. When they got back to the house, his parents were sitting under the pergola, and his father said, 'I see you have shown Bethany where I was shot' he spoke bitterly ' I should have been killed and sometimes I wish I was. People see someone in a wheelchair and will not look into their eyes, as if we are contagious.'

'Oh no, señor!' Bethany squatted down beside the wheelchair and went on, 'My mother died in a car crash when I was sixteen. I was in the car with her when it happened. We had been shopping for a ball dress for me for my high school graduation ball the next week.

'We were so happy, singing in the car to the radio. We stopped at traffic lights which were not far from where we lived. When they turned green, Mother moved off slowly across the road, when a car came zooming through the red lights at great speed. It swerved around us, but the police car chasing it hit our car, killing my mother instantly. I had a badly broken arm and several ribs and was in shock. My physical scars mended quickly, but I was traumatised.

I never got to wear the beautiful ball gown because the day of the ball my mother was buried. I was still recovering in hospital, so I did not get to go to her funeral.

'I have missed my mother every day in every way in the last nine years, so I could imagine how your family would feel if you had died. You have a loving wife and son, and I am sure they feel lucky to have you!'

Señor Rodrigos had tears in his eyes when she finished, and he grasped her hand. 'I am sorry about your mother, Bethany. I do not mean to be ungrateful, as I am aware that I am lucky to have Sofia and Sandro. They have never intimated that I am a burden, and I care for them so very much!'

'As they do you,' Bethany said.

Señora Rodrigos helped her up and held her arms around her and said softly, 'Thank you, Bethany. It is a hard way to learn what a family means. You are very wise, my dear.'

Sandro spoke up with a gruff voice, showing his emotion, 'Time to cheer up! I will get the guitars, and we shall have music.'

'And I will bring the wine and the glasses,' said Sofia.

Sandro came back with two guitars and handed one to his father and then sat down next to Bethany and strummed his guitar. Then looking at her, he played and sang 'La Paloma', a tango and a love song.

After that he sang a cheery song, obviously about horses and riding the range in the moonlight, which his father joined in, and after that went from song to song, and by then everyone was happy again, Bethany revelling in the time and place and the company.

Too soon it was time to move. Sofia had invited Matias and Maria to dinner, so Bethany helped in the kitchen, following orders from Señora Sofia. She liked the farm manager and his wife, thinking they did not deserve a wayward son. They were friendly and down to earth, and although they could not communicate, she watched them through dinner and could see the friendship between the rancher and his manager. Sandro translated anything he thought she might be interested in.

After the couple had returned to their cottage, the dishes were done, and Sandro had helped his father to bed, he took their glasses of wine and her hand and took her to the pergola.

Sandro apologised for the sunset ride, saying he had not been aware of his mother's invitation to the neighbours for dinner. 'I think it was to show you off', he said, laughing. 'I do not bring many girls on our weekends here.'

'Many girls?' she quizzed.

'I brought one once, and she moaned the whole weekend. About "nothing to do" and "It is so quiet" that I have never been tempted again.' He turned to her and said, 'You are so different to any girl I have known before, and I feel so much pleasure each time I am with you.'

'And it is a pleasure to be with you, Sandro. I have enjoyed our time together tremendously.'

He said, 'Shall we go for our ride tomorrow morning to watch the dawn? It is a beautiful time of day. It would be at 6.45 in the morning. Is that too early for you?'

'Certainly not. I am usually an early bird, and it is my favourite time of day. I do admit that I am a little scared about the horse bit, though.'

'Betsy is quite old and staid and a good horse for a beginner, so is it a deal? I will knock on your door at 6 a.m. and will meet you at the stables when you are ready.'

'Yes, it is a deal!'
'Then if we are to get up early in the morning, we had better get some sleep', he said, and holding her hand, they went up the stairs together to their rooms.

****

The next morning went as planned. Bethany apologised for being a scaredy-cat, because the horse Betsy was very gentle, and she found the sensation of riding enjoyable even if it was only a walk. They watched the sun come up, comfortable and quiet in each other's company.

On the way back to the house, she asked, 'Who does Ana look like, Sandro?'

'Our mother, I think. She is very tall for a woman, nearly six foot tall, and has dark shiny hair and big brown eyes, and looks sensual on a catwalk. She is very beautiful. I will show you a magazine in which she featured sometime.'

Bethany asked, 'Did your mother agree with the way your father treated

Ana?'

'My mother always agrees with my father! I think it is because that was the way things were done when they married. The man was head of the house and made all the decisions.'

'Would you expect that of your wife, Sandro?'

'Women seem to be taking over the world as far as I can see, Bethany. Rightly so in many cases. No, I would hope for an amicable relationship with conversations on both sides and decisions made after talking things over.'

'Bravo! Well said! Of course, I am looking at the women's point of view.'

They arrived at the stables to put the horses away, and Betsy nuzzled her as if to say 'You will do.'

In the stables for the main house there was stabling for six horses, though there were only four there at the moment.

In the corner was a tack room and at the other corner stood a carriage that Señor Rodrigos used before his special saddle was devised for his paraplegia. Sandro mentioned that Betsy had pulled the carriage, and if she did not want to ride Betsy, he could dust the carriage down for her!

She laughed and declined the offer, saying she had to ride Betsy now or Sandro would forever call her a 'wimp'.

Coming out of the stable she could see a cottage, surrounded by a privet hedge about 200 yards away – a neat brick and red-tiled house, with a stable at the rear, a garage for their vehicle and an extensive vegetable garden. Everything was very neat and looked like any suburban house, with privacy from the main house. Further over she could see another cottage, possibly workmen quarters, she thought.

Back in the main house, Bethany waited for Sandro to help his father so that they could breakfast together. They left for the city at four o'clock to arrive before dark and dropped her at the hotel first, Sandro saying he would see her at 9 a.m. for breakfast next morning.

She lay on her bed and thought about the weekend. She came to the conclusion that she had never enjoyed herself more. It was the best weekend of her life!

She rang her father in Australia to tell him about her progress so far with the hotel enquiry and about the appointment arranged with Señor Ortega on Tuesday, that if he accepted her offer, she was going to purchase the hotel.

She told him about the weekend at the ranch and how much she had enjoyed it. He sounded fascinated when she was describing Sandro; he had not heard her so enthusiastic since the death of her mother and wondered if Sandro was the cause of it.

Chapter 5

Next morning at breakfast she found Sandro somewhat subdued. She searched her mind to see if she could find the reason for it, but could not think of anything.

After they had eaten, they set off for the Plaza de Mayo as Sandro had promised.

They spent some time reading all the notices around the plaza, then strolled down some side streets, looking at the boutique shops. They came to a large white church where an early Mass had just finished and worshippers were just leaving as they entered. The church was impressive inside and quiet, as it was too early for tourists to be looking around. They wandered around for ten minutes and then Sandro motioned to a seat and they sat down.

They were quiet for a while and then Sandro said in a quiet voice, 'My family has been registered in this church for over one hundred years, and if you would marry me, we could be married at that altar.'

She looked at him, not quite sure she had understood what he had said. He looked back, not saying anymore.

She thought about what she had thought he said and then spoke. 'Is that a marriage proposal?'

'Yes, I love you, Bethany. You have taken over my mind. I cannot concentrate because I just want to be with you. I love everything about you, your calm voice, your courtesy, your friendly manner, your whole personality, and into the bargain, you are beautiful. You are everything a man could ever want, and I want you to be my wife.' He paused and then went on, 'I know it has been just over a week, but in that week we have spent most of our time together, morning, noon, and evening, and I want to have breakfast with you every morning for the rest of our lives, preferably after a long night of love. I love you, Bethany!'

He went on, 'I spoke to my parents last night, about proposing to you, and they encouraged me. My father said that life can be short, and we should take this opportunity as you will go back to Australia and we may never meet again. We will have missed out on a lifetime of love and happiness if I do not at least ask you!'

'Sandro, that sounds like good reasoning to me, but there are a few things I should tell you about myself before I answer your proposal and then you can ask me again if you want.

'Firstly, I do love you. I have tried to deny that to myself, saying it's a holiday romance and such. But I know I do. After the weekend at the ranch, I came back to the quiet of the hotel and probed my feelings, and yes, I love you!

'There may be a complication for you though, so I had better tell you now and see if it makes any difference to you. The "Company" trying to take over your hotel is my company. When my mother died, she had two Life Insurance policies, one for death and one for accidental death, and I was named as beneficiary in both of them.

'Also, my father is a lawyer, and the last thing you would want to do is kill the lawyer's wife and injure his child and be in the wrong about it. He sued on my behalf, and I was awarded a very large sum of money. This money has been invested for me over the last nine years and so I am able to purchase the Hotel Aria tomorrow if I want and Señor Ortega agrees to sell to me. Do you still want to marry me?'

'Wow! Bethany, I must say you continue to surprise me! I don't know what to say.' He paused and went on, 'It does not change the fact that we love each other. We will work something out.' There was silence for a few minutes. 'You have not said you will marry me yet. Please say yes or no and put me out of my misery.'

'Yes, Sandro! Yes yes, I love you, and I will marry you!'
He put his arms around her. 'I can hardly believe it! I was afraid you would laugh at me. I have wanted to hold you since we first met. I have never felt like this before. You are so beautiful, my darling. You have made me so happy!'

'Let us get out of here. It is so cold. I need a cup of coffee.'

They found a small coffee house and sat over their coffee for some time. Sandro asked whether, after telling his parents the good news, she would mind if he rang Señor Ortega to tell the news. 'He has been like a father to me. When my father was too ill to be a father to me, he stepped in and helped me so much, and this news may brighten him up a little.'

'Certainly', she said. 'I am not too sure if he knows that I am the person negotiating with him tomorrow and not a conglomerate. You had better tell him that too. I would not like him to have a heart attack in the middle of negotiations.'

They decided to go and tell his parents and then he would take her to the hotel so she could tell her father in private. She was not too sure how her family would take it.

Her father listened to her and said, 'You had better take a lawyer with you tomorrow and insist that Señor Ortega is represented as well, to witness as the gentleman is so ill. You do not want anything to go wrong, so you must tie things up properly.'

He made no comment on the wedding proposal, probably because he wanted to think it over.

He had a point, of course. About a lawyer.
So, Bethany went for a walk until she came to a lawyer's office and knocked on the door. She was relieved when a middle-aged man answered and welcomed her in.

She first asked if he spoke English and was pleased when he said that he did. She explained her position to him and was relieved when he agreed to represent her.

He made a few calls to clear his day and then asked her to take him through all the details again.

He agreed to meet her the next morning at the Hotel Aria for breakfast and go with Sandro to the designated appointment.

****

At breakfast the next morning she explained that the lawyer, Señor Francis Lazar, would be arriving soon to represent her.

Sandro explained that Señor Ortega had asked if he would come with her as well, to the meeting.

38

He also said that Señor Lazar had a good reputation, and he thought it a good idea and appropriate to have representation because there would be Spanish in the paperwork for official reasons. It was a big transaction. And to have someone to explain legalities to her was really needed.

Bethany rang her father to give him Señor Lazar's telephone number in case he had any questions and said she would give her father's number to the lawyer.

She felt satisfied with all this, and when the lawyer arrived, they had breakfast and then Sandro drove them to Señor Ortega's residence, a large house not far from the hotel.

****

Señora Ortega answered the door, kissed Sandro, and welcomed Bethany and Señor Lazar. She took Sandro's arm and showed them into the salon where the señor sat in an armchair.

Standing nearby were a lawyer and his clerk. After the introductions, they sat down opposite Señor Ortega, and he began, saying, 'Welcome, Señorita Fordham. You have begun well by capturing the heart of our beloved Sandro. Now let us see if you can capture my mind by bartering the Hotel Aria with me. The hotel has been part of my life as long as I can remember.'

'You advertised a price, señor, and that is exactly the amount that I have in my company account, and for the Hotel Aria, I am willing to pay that to you in American dollars.'

Señor Ortega raised his eyebrows and said, 'No bartering, señorita?'
To this she answered, 'I had intended to barter with you, señor, before I arrived in Buenos Aires, but Sandro has told me how kind you have been to him over a long time and how much you have taught him, and he loves you as if you were his father, so I cannot barter with you.'

He looked at her for a long moment, then at Sandro. 'OK, then I will make a deal with you. If you marry Sandro within a month, I will take half the sum you are willing to pay. This will be for half the hotel. The other half I will put into Sandro's name.

'My wife and I have discussed this overnight, and we agree we wish to give Sandro something, for we love him like a son. This seems a solution to us, and our lawyers have drawn up an agreement if you agree to these terms. Should the marriage not go ahead, you may purchase the hotel in your name, and we shall think of an alternative for Sandro.

'I am hoping for an agreement now, as I have been told by my doctors that time is of the essence to complete my will if the hotel is not sold. My lawyer has the agreement, and if you would like your lawyer to study it now, we can come to a happy agreement.'

The lawyers studied the papers together, and Señor Ortega went on, 'I know some refurbishment is necessary at the hotel. I thought the new owners would like to change things to their way. That is why the property is not overpriced, so you could use the money saved to do what you like.'

'I am also leaving to Sandro the apartment adjoining the hotel. It is on a different title. I have used this as my own place, and sometimes special guests have been billeted there.'

Bethany looked at Sandro, who looked absolutely stunned, and at her lawyer, who nodded to her and said, 'A wonderful deal, señorita, if you intend to marry Señor Rodrigos!'

'He looks better by the minute!' she said and turned back to Sandro and asked if he was happy with what Señor Ortega proposed.

He came alive and hugged her and then went over to the Ortegas and hugged them both.

'Thank you for your faith in me', he said to them. 'I will endeavour to live up to your expectations of me and the memory of you and the Hotel Aria forever.' The lawyers had finished studying the agreement and said everything was in order and so the signing began.

Señora Ortega brought some wine and glasses to the table, and toasts were made. As they were leaving, Señor Ortega gave Sandro the keys he had of the hotel and also the keys to the apartment. He wished them a happy life and happiness and kissed him.

Tears came to Sandro's eyes, and he gently hugged back and kissed him on the cheek.

The older man then turned to Bethany. He kissed her and then thanked her for her earlier kind words and said, 'You are getting a good man as husband, señorita. Treat him well. He is very special to us.'

****

After returning Señor Lazar to his office, where he would copy the documents and lodge them with the right officials and return them the next day, Sandro took Bethany to the luxury apartment to show her. It appeared as an appendage to the hotel but was on a different title.

On the dining room table was a basket of fruit, wine and savouries wrapped up in cellophane, with a note, reading, 'Hola, Sandro, you have won yourself a beautiful bride!'

Sandro laughed. 'Señor Ortega was always one step ahead of me!'
He took Bethany into his arms and said, 'At last! I get to hold you! How often I have wanted to do this! Since I saw you first, I held back in case you pushed me away.'

'I would not have pushed you away, Sandro. I think I fell in love you when you blushed at the airport.'

'And I fell in love with you when you walked through the airport like a ray of sunshine on a foggy day.'

He kissed her, and the kiss turned into a long journey in sensations.
'Bethany, I would like to make love to you. Do you want to wait till our wedding night?'

'You kiss me like that and expect me to wait a month for the next chapter? Oh no, Sandro, I love you and cannot wait!'

He picked her up in his arms and walked to the bedroom, kissing her until they arrived at the king-size bed.

****

41

Later that afternoon, Sandro reluctantly said, 'I must go and tend my father, and now I have surfaced I find I am very hungry. Let's go and tell my parents about our good news. I am sure that they are expecting us because I have not telephoned to say we are not coming.'

They showered together and dried themselves on the big fluffy towels provided and dressed and went back to the world.

Chapter 6

How happy his parents and grandmother were for them, with Sandro telling them in Spanish, as his grandmother did not know English, apologising to Bethany.

'I must hurry and have some Spanish lessons', she said in reply.
'So, Bethany, you are really going to join our family?' asked Señora Sofia.
'Yes, señora, I will be happy to join your family as your daughter-in-law. I love you almost as much as I love Sandro.'

Everyone cheered at this and hugged her.

'There is one favour I would ask of you, Señora Sofia. Will you help me to prepare for the wedding? I know nothing of the way things are done in Argentina, so I will need a lot of help so as not to upset anyone.'

Señora Sofia's eyes lit up, and she hugged Bethany once again.

'It will bring me much pleasure. You will make a beautiful bride. We have only one month to carry out Señor Ortega's wishes, so we had better start tomorrow. Grandmother will be a big help. She knows so many officials. It should make things easier and quicker.'

Bethany turned to Grandmother and held her hand whilst Señora Sofia explained to her what was happening.

Grandmother beamed and said, 'Si señorita, Maniana.'

Bethany explained that the lawyer was coming in the morning, but she would come as soon as he had gone.

Sandro came to her and told her he would help his father to bed, but he would be as quick as possible so that he could take her back to the hotel.

Sofia went with her husband, so Bethany and Grandmother cleared the table and washed the dishes.

When Sandro returned, they went out to the car, and he asked whether she wanted to go to the apartment or to the hotel.

'My heart says apartment, but my head tells me hotel. The lawyer is coming in the morning, and we could use clear heads to see him and did not want him and the staff see them flushed with a night of love. It would be very entertaining for the staff.'

He drove her to the hotel and walked her to her room and kissed her goodnight.

The next morning Señor Lazar arrived sharply at nine o'clock with their copies of the papers they had signed the previous day.

He had rung her father the previous evening and explained the details of the proceedings and expected her father to ring her if he had any concerns. He then reminded her that she had one month to change her mind!

Bethany looked at Sandro across the table. 'I will not change my mind, señor.'

'The same goes for you too, Sandro', said the lawyer.
'Señor, I asked Bethany to marry me before all these proceedings began, and I am satisfied our love for each other will last. I am grateful to Señor Ortega for what he has done for me, but it makes no difference to my love for Bethany and hers for me.'

'Good! Well, we have got that out of the way, and the next subject is visas. Miss Randford will have a six-month visitor visa, and if she is to stay here as your wife, this must be rectified through the immigration department. Do you want me to represent you there?'

'Yes, please, señor. Do you need my passport?'
'Only the details from it for a start. Never give anyone your passport, especially a stranger, señorita.'

'I am sure I can trust you. But I know what you mean. There are some circumstances where it is necessary.'

'I will lodge an application with a copy of the hotel agreement, and hopefully there will not be too much delay.'

'Today we are going to organise a wedding,' she said, 'and this afternoon I will move into Sandro's apartment to give us some privacy, as I am sure the staff are all agog wondering what is going on, and we must put their minds at rest about their jobs.'

****

The next three weeks went in a whirl of dress fittings. Elena was to be bridesmaid and her little daughter Elle was to be the flower girl. Elena had extended her stay to attend the wedding and would fly back home with Bethany's family a few days after it.

Bethany's dress was beautiful with a long lacy veil. Elena and Elle's dresses were the same as hers, but in a peach shade that went well with their dark hair.

The reception was to be held in the Hotel Aria's ballroom. Sandro was organising that and caterers were coming in for the meal. Invitations had gone out via the Rodrigos family to a lot of people she did not know, but best of all, Bethany's father and his wife Jenny and their little boy, Mathew, had arrived and were staying in the apartment with her. Her brother Mark and his wife Laura had arrived from the USA, where Mark was doing a fellowship in Atlanta, Georgia, before returning home to practise in Australia. She had organised a room in the hotel for them.

A photographer had been hired for the day – photographs for before she left for the church and during the service and at the reception.

Bethany had been coaxed by Señora Sofia and Grandmother to give the right answers in Spanish at the right time during the service.

****

And then the day had arrived! She felt so nervous as Jenny and Laura and Elena helped her to get dressed, but a lot of laughing put her at ease at last. The wedding was to be held at 5.30 p.m. after the tourists had all gone for the day.

After the photographer had finished, she was on her way with her father in a limousine. The others had gone on ahead.

'Are you sure, Bethany', her father asked.

'Yes, Dad, as sure as anything in my life.' He sighed and said, 'Well, I like your Sandro, and everyone seems to think well of him. We will miss you. It is not like just driving half an hour down the road to see you.'

'Thank you for coming, Dad. It is a big help having you here. I will miss you too, and I promise to ring you at least once a week.'

Then they were there and entered the church to the organ playing the wedding march. The church was full, and she felt nervous as she walked down the aisle on her father's arm. It seemed a long aisle!

She smiled at her family in the front seats and at the Rodrigos family, with Señor Ortega and his wife beside him with their glowing smiles.

And then she saw Sandro looking at her, and her heart said, 'Yes!'

She answered in all the right places in the ceremony in Spanish, and they were married!

Sandro leaned over to her and said softly, 'You are beautiful, Señora Rodrigos, and I am happy to be your husband.'

And she replied, 'I am happy to be your wife, Señor Rodrigos', and she kissed him to the clapping of the congregation.

The walk down the aisle did not seem so bad with Sandro to hold on to.

****

The reception at the Hotel Aria was magnificent. All the staff stood in line to receive them, clapping their hands, followed by guitar players strumming the wedding march. Being seated by Sandro and Daniel at the main table was quite a ceremony.

Sandro had ordered the wedding decorations – white-backed chairs with big bows on the back, candelabrum on each table, and white flowers down the centre. It was really lovely. The staff had done a wonderful job. Special cutlery and crystal glasses finished it off nicely.

She murmured to Sandro, 'I think we have found a reason to use the ballroom more often. What you have done here is magnificent enough to start a new trend in weddings, and this is a wonderful venue.'

Sandro grinned and said, 'I see I have married a hard-headed businesswoman! You are right. We are now free to do what we want with the hotel. I think, though, that we should wait until Señor Ortega is gone before we start changing things, and this could be our first change.'

Señor Ortega had not joined them for the reception, as he was now too frail. At midnight the crowd had begun to thin. Many people had a long way to go home, so the bride and groom went upstairs to change clothes and then departed with cheers from the remaining crowd.

They were going for the night to the large hotel where they had dinner in the first week of Bethany's arrival in Buenos Aires. The next morning, they were going to the ranch, after checking that the nurse they had arranged for Sandro's father was in place.

They were staying a week at the ranch as their honeymoon. Bethany's family were coming to the ranch for a day mid week before flying to Australia next day.

When her dad saw the ranch, he said, 'What a wonderful location for holiday chalets! So peaceful and beautiful!'

Bethany looked at Sandro for his response, because she had thought the exact same thing on her first visit here. She had not thought it her place to promote it.

'Yes,' said Sandro. 'Many of our neighbours let out rooms to tourists. I do not know of any chalet-type accommodation, but it was the peace and quiet that the family liked, and at this stage we do not want to share the place. However, who knows in the future what may happen.'

Everyone agreed with that sentiment. They were sitting around the table, and Bethany felt proud of her first attempt at entertaining as a wife.

She was sorry to see her family leave, not knowing when they would see each other again. She clung to her father until Sandro lifted her away and held her by his side until they had left her sight.

She could not contain her sobs once they had gone, and Sandro held her close until she blew her nose and sniffed. 'I am sorry, Sandro. I did not think it would be so hard to say goodbye. We have always been a close-family unit. I am sorry too that my grandparents did not come to the wedding. They would have loved it, but they decided they could not sit for such a long time in the aircraft because of Granddad's bad knees.'

'We will visit them as soon as it is possible. There is nothing wrong with our knees, my love, and we will go together.'

Bethany could not feel down too long when she was with Sandro and said, 'It is almost sunset. Let's go for our ride. Betsy will be looking for me.'

Betsy had taken Bethany as her own and snickered as soon as she appeared. They had been riding morning and evening, and she felt quite confident now.

Sandro admired how she looked on the horse and said, 'You are a natural on a horse. You will be playing polo soon.'

'Polo? You play polo, Sandro?'
'Yes, usually in winter. It is too hot for the horses in summer. I play with the local team each fortnight when we come to the ranch. It is a very exciting game. I will take you to a game when it starts up again in the city. That is an exciting game! Argentina is well up in the world for their polo.'

'I am still learning of your skills, Sandro. I will never tire of you at the rate you keep surprising me with new things.'

'On the way to the city, when we leave tomorrow, we will go via a town called San Antonio de Areco. It is popular with tourists because of the gauchos in their colourful scarves and their berets. You can see the gaucho or cowboy riding in the paddocks, and they will wave to you. We can stay at an estancia overnight before returning home.'

'Sounds wonderful! I am curious about the estancias, I must say, although I agree with you that it is not right for the Rodrigos family. This ranch has been a perfect honeymoon place, with no one to please but ourselves. I am not promoting it for anyone else. It is so good and just for us!'

'Sandro, how come you haven't been snapped up by an Argentine beauty by now? You are twenty-eight, tall, dark, and handsome and charming into the bargain. Has there been a long line of contestants for the role of your wife knocking on your door?'

Sandro roared with laughter.

'You have a wonderful turn of phrase, Señora. I have taken a few ladies out and even got close to proposing to one girl. I asked Señor Ortega for his opinion of her, and his remark stuck in my head. I knew what he meant when I met you!'

'What was the remark?'
'He said that if I needed someone else's opinion, then it was not the right person, and I should wait until I knew it was right. He was a wise man, and I always listened to his advice, and so, my darling, I have you instead of an Argentine beauty. And I am very happy I waited. It was just like he said. I knew immediately you were the right wife for me!'

They were reluctant to pack up. It had been a magic week, and the next time they came back to the ranch would be accompanied by Sandro's parents.

But Betsy would be waiting for her daily walks again.

****

The hotel was waiting for them, and they had organised a full staff meeting on Monday to tell the staff of the new management arrangements.

Bethany had already moved her things into Sandro's house, so it was an exciting future for them.

Chapter 7

They went to the hotel on Monday for breakfast at nine o'clock, and as they walked in the door, the staff were assembled in the foyer and clapped them into the hotel. They were thrilled. Both felt it was a very special moment to be received like this. They invited everyone into the breakfast room for pastries and coffee. Sandro told them that the ownership of the hotel had shifted to him and his wife.

There was silence for a few moments as this information was digested and then Daniel led the others into congratulations.

Sandro told them there would be no change of staff and that in the next week there would be a small raise in pay for everyone.

Should they have any comments, they should speak to either Señor or Señora Rodrigos, and they would be listened to, as they were the ones doing the work and so knew what was needed. 'Are there any questions now?'

There was a silence for a moment, with everyone looking at each other until Daniel spoke up.

'Thank you, Sandro. We sort of guessed that something was happening, but this has surprised us all. We welcome you back with us, and we will carry on as usual.'

Bethany then spoke. 'There is one more thing I would like to say. I have been here some time now, and I have noticed that it is a very quiet hotel, no sound of laughter or chatter. I would like to think that you enjoy your time here with us, so unless it is disturbing a guest, which we must never do, then I would like you to sing, be happy, and most of all, be friendly! It will make a big difference to your time here.'

Sandro was amazed at this and said, 'You think this will make a difference, señora?'

'Yes, señor. I like a happy home, and the quietness here unsettles me. I do not want loudness, just happiness. A smile is a wonderful thing to share and can make a big difference to the one you smile at.'

Everybody was smiling and saying 'Si, si señora' in happy tones.

After Sandro had dismissed them to go about their work, he looked at her in admiration. 'And all that in Spanish! You surprise me now! You are right. Señor Ortega never liked the staff chatting. It was the old way that the staff had been treated here, and as we are going to make some changes, this is a good way to start!'

The next thing they did was to ring the Ortega house to see how the señor was doing. His wife answered the phone and said, 'As good as can be expected. He was very frail now and sleeping more and more, but if you would like to visit him, I will make sure he is up to receive you. I know he would like to welcome you home.'

Bethany rang Señor Lazar, the lawyer, and asked if their settlement papers for the hotel were ready for them to pick up from his office.

He said, 'Congratulations! Yes, all is ready. However, I am due in court in fifteen minutes, but my secretary will give you the package if you want to come now.'

As they walked down the street, Bethany had to resist skipping, though she could not resist smiling. Sandro noticed her and said, 'You are the smiliest person I have ever met, and life is so good now with you by my side, I cannot stop smiling too.'

She said, 'Six weeks ago, I lived alone in another country. By a sudden whim when I saw an advertisement in a hotel magazine, I flew to this country. I am now an Argentine, married to an incredible man, and the owner of half a hotel, and still have money in my account. How smiley is that?'

Señor Ortega was sitting in his armchair when they arrived at two o'clock. He was ashen but alert. Sandro kissed the older man and held his hand and told him they had picked up the deeds to the hotel and the apartment from the lawyer and expressed all his thanks for all the things Señor Ortega had done for him.

Bethany stepped forward and said, 'I believe I have you to thank for keeping Sandro unmarried and looking for me.'

The old man chuckled and said, 'I was always ready to advise and didn't expect people to follow my advice, but Sandro was a good student. I am delighted with your happiness, both of you, and you have my heartfelt wishes that you will always feel as happy as you feel today.'

They felt they had to leave, as he looked so tired, so they both kissed him on the cheek and wished him well.

Sandro went once more the next week and came home saying he thought it would be the last he would see of him.

Señora Ortega rang early the following morning to say her husband died in his sleep during the night. She had found him with a peaceful smile on his face. He would be interred in the family mausoleum at the Recoleta Cemetery early next week.

Bethany had not been to the Recoleta Cemetery previously, and when they arrived to follow the Ortega cortege, she was astounded to see all the mausoleums, so different to the cemetery at home. It looked like a village with the streets aligned and large family mausoleums both sides of the streets, which wound around.

Sandro supported Señora Ortega, and Bethany walked beside them. There were no sign of the daughters, to farewell their father, but the crowd that followed the cortege showed he had been a popular man.

He was laid to rest with his parents, in the family mausoleum.

Just a month later, Bethany woke up feeling unwell and realised that she had missed her courses for three weeks and was probably pregnant. She woke Sandro to tell him the news, and he was ecstatic. 'Can we tell my parents and grandmother right away?'

'I think we should have it confirmed by a doctor first, then invite them to lunch at a restaurant to celebrate, as I cannot bear the thought of preparing food at the moment as I feel so nauseated.'

The family were all pleased at the news. There were probably no babysitting problems here!

Her pregnancy went well. The morning sickness stopped at three months, and she was admitted to a private hospital when her pains started for the delivery. Twelve hours later she was holding a seven-pound baby boy with dark hair and what looked like brown eyes.

They named their son Robert Phillipe after the two grandfathers. He was a pretty baby, and it turned out he had the same calm manner as Sandro. There was rarely crying in the house.

Sofia and grandmother were always happy to look after him when Bethany had to go to the hotel or go shopping. He was the central figure in the house. He walked at eleven months, and when they went to the ranch, Sandro would put him on the front of him on the horse, and he loved it. His talking was a bit slower; it seemed he was listening to Spanish and English and working them out in his head to see which language was best.

He was a happy child, and Bethany spent most of her time with him, as she did not seem to be needed at the hotel. Sandro was spending more and more time at the hotel, and she wished sometimes that he would spend more time at home with her and Robert, as he rarely saw Robert who was asleep when he came home from tending his father and left to tend his father again in the morning before Robert was awake.

She was starting to resent the time Sandro spent with his parents, but as she had accepted it when they were married, she did not know what to do about it; meanwhile she felt Robert made up a lot to her.

She and Sandro were still very happy in each other's company when he was home, but she did miss outside occupation. She had been a busy businesswoman before her marriage and felt as if she was being left behind. She did not blame Robert's arrival. She loved him too much for that. But it was a long day with only an almost two-year-old to talk to and keep her busy. She had suggested to Sandro that she return some days to the hotel to expand her mind, but he had laughingly put her off, saying her mind was beautiful as it was! He laughed at her discontent by saying she was beautiful as well as smart and Robert would benefit with such a full-time mother looking after him!

Chapter 8

Because the garden at the units was so small, Bethany took Robert by the hand and walked to the nearby park. He enjoyed playing with the other children, and Bethany liked to chat with the other mothers and nursemaids. Her Spanish was quite good. She had practised it in the shops and in the hotel and had got proficient in it. Robert loved the outing and always took a toy with him to play with. It had become a ritual with them, and they would stay in the park for about an hour each time they went.

On Robert's second birthday, Bethany realised that she may be pregnant again. She had not told Sandro, as he had rushed out of the house early. Also, she wanted a doctor's confirmation first.

Robert and Bethany went for their usual walk to the park with Bethany videoing on her iPhone to send a record back to her family in Australia of the birthday.

As they walked towards the park, she noticed a white van idling near the park gate. It was a 'No parking' area, which is why she noticed it, but then gave no more attention to it, as she was busy with her videoing.

There was a woman ahead of her standing by the van, so Bethany picked up Robert to avoid her. As she picked up Robert to do this, a man, who had been walking behind her, appeared and grabbed Robert from her arms. She screamed, but the man jumped into the van with Robert, with the woman in the driver's seat, and they took off around the corner and were gone!

She screamed Robert's name and tried to chase the van, but it had disappeared too fast for her.

She phoned Sandro, crying into the phone, and he was there within minutes. She realised that the man had thrust an envelope into her hands, and she gave it to Sandro when she realised it had his name on it. She could not stop crying. 'Robert is gone! A man stole Robert and drove away!'

'Look, Sandro, I took a video of it. This is the man and the woman. I had the camera on to photograph Robert, and I caught them on film taking him!'

Sandro looked at the video and said, 'That is Miguel, much older, but Miguel unmistakable.'

' What does the letter say?' Bethany asked

He opened it and read quickly and then handed it to her, and she read.

'I will look after your son, but I need $300,00 US right away. I will phone your wife and let her know where to meet me. If your wife brings me cash for this amount by tomorrow noon, I will hand the boy over to her. Do not call the police or you will not see your son again. PS: It is not for drugs. Signed Miguel.'

Sandro said in a dead voice, 'You gave Robert to Miguel.'

'No no, Sandro! He snatched Robert from my arms! How could I know who Miguel was? I have never seen him before today he is a complete stranger to me, and he grabbed Robert from me! I could not stop him!'

Her husband looked at her as if he loathed her. 'You had better get the money ready for tomorrow.'

Back at the house when Sandro told his parents about it, they all looked at Bethany as if she had planned it all.

She felt so ill and depressed from crying so much, she went to bed and took a sleeping tablet. When she awoke next morning, Sandro was gone.

She was getting ready to go to the bank, when there was a knock on the door. Sofia had let into the courtyard, one of the neighbouring mothers and nursemaid Rosa, whom she often talked to at the park.

Rosa explained that she had seen the kidnapping the previous day, and she had recognised the woman with the man who had taken Robert as one of her mother's neighbours. She knew where they lived!

Bethany hugged her and said, 'We will go together as soon as I have been to the bank to get the money they have asked for. I will come back, and we shall go together. Thank you, Rosa!'

The next knock on the door was Matias and Maria. Sandro had phoned them the previous evening, and they had driven to the house to see if there was anything they could do.

'Yes, Matias, you stay here with my parents-in-law and try to keep things calm. Maria, you come with me and we will go and try to see Miguel.'

The bank gave her the money asked for in a plastic bag, and she marvelled that such a small package could save her son's life.

She felt calm and in control, but knew that she could not keep it up if things started to go wrong. But she did not have Sandro's support and felt the loss of it dreadfully. She could not understand why Sandro was so detached, as if he did not know her and Robert. She felt inconsolable about it but knew she had to stay calm while trying to rescue Robert, he was her first concern and she had to keep her wits about her so tried not to think of Sandro and his strange distance he had drawn between them.

The three women drove to Rosa's mother's home and quizzed her on whether she had noticed anything out of place. But no, she had seen the children playing in the street, but there were always children and had not taken particular notice; she was not aware of any kidnapping, so did not look for a strange child.

The white van was parked at the kerb of the house across the road, so the three women used it for shelter as they crossed the road and were unseen by the people in the house where Miguel held her son.

Bethany knocked at the door and could hear Robert's squeal of laughter from beyond it in the house.

As the door opened, she could see Robert playing in the passageway with three other children.

'I have come for my son, Señor Miguel!'
He looked completely taken aback. 'Señora Rodrigos!' Then he looked past her to his mother.

'Come in', he said. 'Your son is safe. He is a brave little boy, and no harm has come to him. I think he has enjoyed his stay with us.' Miguel held his mother close.

Pushing herself away from her son, his mother ran to the children, saying, 'Are these my grandchildren, Miguel?'

'Yes, Mama, I needed money for my eldest son's back so that he can walk, which has led me to do this dishonourable thing against the Rodrigos family. I am deeply sorry, Señora Rodrigos, but I have been forced by circumstances to do this thing to you.

'I never left Buenos Aires after leaving the ranch. I just laid low. I knew the police were looking for me. I got a job in this area and married and have been here ever since leaving.

'When I came down from the high, I was on from drugs that day I shot your father-in-law, I was so ashamed that I have never taken alcohol or drugs since then. My wife helped me yesterday because we are both exhausted over our son and felt we had no alternative!'

Bethany looked at him for some time. 'I wish to see your son, Miguel.'

He showed her into a bedroom where a young lad lay on the bed. He was about ten years old. It was obvious that he could not move, and his mother sat on a chair next to him.

Bethany looked at Miguel, and her face was impassive as she said, 'The sins of the father are visited on the son.' She paused. 'You will have the money to help your son to walk, but my father-in-law will never walk again.'

She handed the bag of money to Miguel with a stony face, walked out of the room to where Robert played, and picked him up.

She turned to Maria and said, 'Stay here, Maria. Get to know your grandchildren, and I will send your husband to you.'

She drove the car with Rosa and Robert back to their home and gave Rosa $100 US, saying, 'Thank you, Rosa. Without you it may not have worked out so well. I will forever be grateful to you.'

When she arrived at the Rodrigos home, she told the family what had happened and gave Matias the address to find Maria.

Sofia and Phillipe Rodrigos both gazed at Bethany and said, 'You really gave Miguel money, Bethany?'

'Yes, I did, not for Miguel but for the boy in need of operations to his back. I could not refuse.'

Their faces showed that mercy did not figure in their minds, and Bethany felt they held it against her. The fact that Robert had been returned seemed not to have to be acknowledged!

She went back to Sandro's house and rang him to let him know what had happened, and his reaction was the same as his parents, but even more disbelieving of her good intentions!

She felt absolutely astonished at their attitude and could not get over that the fact of Robert's return was not of any consequence.

Later that evening, when Sandro had come home, he said he would move out to the apartment, as he could not believe her story.

Bethany stared at him, unable to believe what was happening, and then said, 'If anyone is to move out, it should be me, as you are needed here to attend your father. I will take Robert with me. He has had a traumatic experience, so he needs his mother's attention.'

She went slowly upstairs and packed Robert's clothes and then packed for herself, not knowing how long to pack for. She asked Sandro to carry Robert downstairs and put him in his car seat, and she took the bags.

Sandro was quiet while he did this and did not say anything more as she drove away.

The apartment was used for a luxury stay for those that could afford it but was not being used for the moment. She put Robert to bed and sat with him till he went to sleep and then stared into space, trying to work out what she had done wrong!

She was unable to work it out and decided that she was not at fault. She had done nothing wrong.

It was like a Sicilian revenge story! Of course, Sandro was half Sicilian.
She had got Robert back from Miguel; he was not damaged!

It was her money paid for a young child's operations to help him walk!

But it was her now sitting in the apartment without her husband! And her husband's family that she now thought of as her own family!

What a mess! She could not get her mind around it. Perhaps tomorrow things will return to normal when they have had time to think about it.

However, when she tried to ring Sandro next morning, she found the phone blocked to her. She took Robert for breakfast at the hotel, but Sandro did not appear. She tried ringing him again, but she was still blocked out.

She had a doctor's appointment the next day and had to take Robert with her, so the nurse played with him whilst the doctor examined her and confirmed her pregnancy. She asked the doctor to send a report of the pregnancy to Sandro.

She tried to ring Sandro again without result, so she tried Señora Sofia with the same result. They were blackballing her! She was nonplussed.

She did not know what to do. It was so unexpected that she felt lost. On the third day when there had been no contact with Sandro, she rang Señor Lazar and made an appointment. She felt she had no one else to turn to. She had been here for such a short time and had been so engrossed with her husband and son and the Rodrigos family, she had not made friends she could talk to and help her.

When the appointment time came, she went with Robert and explained what had happened, apologising to the lawyer for laying it all before him, saying, 'I do not want to ring my family in Australia yet, because I do not think they would understand', as she certainly didn't.

The lawyer listened to her story and looked pensive for a while and said that the family was obviously traumatised by what had happened so many years ago and felt she had helped the man who had caused that trauma.

'Perhaps if you go home to Australia to your family and see if Sandro misses you and Robert and come to collect you. It would give the family more time to come to terms with the situation. However, to take Robert out of the country, you will need to have Sandro's permission.'

His calm reasoning voice stopped the panic that had kept coming over her, and she agreed to his suggestion and asked him if he would approach Sandro, as he would not talk to her. She also told him she was pregnant and asked if he would tell her husband as well.

She expected Sandro to come and give his permission, but he gave the permission to the lawyer for her to take Robert out of the country.

She was astounded. Just like that! She no longer mattered to him. She felt it had been a dream, but she had Robert to prove it had been real! Even Robert seemed nothing to him! How could it all be true! The love they had for each other must have only been a dream for it to end like this.

Before she left the lawyer's office, Señor Lazar suggested that she give a statement regarding the kidnapping, saying it may be needed in the future. So she went through it all over again with him and showed him the photos of Miguel and his wife at the park, the white van, and the photos she had taken on her phone while Miguel was not looking of him and his wife and children and Mother, of the boy in the bed and the money which she gave for him. She also had the ransom note. She dialled up on her phone to show the bank statement of the money withdrawn on that day. She also mentioned that Rosa's mother had recognised Maria as a woman she had seen many times visiting the house across the road! He took copies of it all, and she signed a statement with his secretary as witness.

The next day, Sandro was still not answering his phone, so she decided to take the lawyer's advice and go to Australia. She rang the airline and made a reservation and visited immigration to have Robert included on her passport along with the letter allowing him to leave the country with her

They left for Australia the next day. She felt so sad. Sandro had said many times that they would visit Australia together for her to see her family, but she was going without him. Somehow, he just did not want them anymore; it seemed worse than if he had died. She felt bereft.

Chapter 9

Her family was very glad to see them. They were mystified at Sandro's attitude. How could things go so badly so quickly?

After a few weeks staying with her father and Jenny, Robert was getting on very well with his small uncle Mathew. She was able to move back to her own town house, which had been rented out during her absence, in Argentina. She felt completely at a loss at first, but gradually accepted that she was alone again to manage her pregnancy.

She kept healthy by walking every day, taking Robert with her in a jogging pram, until she was too heavy to jog and dropped back to walking. She made sure that they both ate well. Time passed slowly at first.

Robert often asked at the beginning when were they going home. He missed his grandparents and father at first, but stopped asking after a while. Small children forgot so quickly.

He was learning to speak so much better. She spoke to him in Spanish as well as English, and he was quickly becoming bilingual without thinking about it. He was a very bright little boy.

He especially loved it when they visited Grandfather Robert so he could play with his almost five-year-old uncle Mathew. Towards the end of her pregnancy Bethany and Robert moved back to her father's house so that he could take her to the maternity hospital when her time came, so Jenny could look after Robert.

During her time then at her father's house, she brought up the subject of divorce and having custody of the children.

There had been no contact from Sandro for eight months since she had left his house.

Her father suggested they contact Señor Lazar to find out about Argentines' laws on divorce, so they rang the lawyer straightaway. He promised to get back to them.

****

Two days later, she went into labour and a little girl was born at 3 a.m. on Bethany's twenty-eighth birthday.

69

She looked at the tiny baby, only six lbs. and thought, 'This baby is really mine. We shall share birthdays, and she will never know her father.' She sobbed so hard the nurses became concerned for her. She waved them away. No one could help her, but she was intent that she would make it up to her baby for the loss of a father.

The doctor was so concerned for her state of mind that he gave an injection to help her to sleep and recover.

When she opened her eyes next, she was in her bed with the baby in a cot beside her. Bethany was only half awake but could sense someone sitting beside her.

She turned her head and saw Sandro. She felt very confused for a while, then saw that it really was Sandro sitting there and holding her hand. She snatched her hand back and turned to go to sleep again as if it had been a bad dream.

'Hola, Bethany,' he said, 'our little girl is beautiful and looks just like you.'

She turned her head back to him. 'That little girl is my little girl! All you did was plant the seed. I nurtured her all alone, so she is not yours, she is mine!'

She thought for a moment and said, 'Have you seen Robert yet?'

'Yes, I went to your father's house straight from the airport, and he led Robert to me. He is very grown up now.'

'Yes, he has grown up now and you have missed eight months of his life. Did he know you?'

Sandro gave an apologetic smile. 'No, he did not. All he wanted to do was go back to play with Mathew, his little uncle.'

'Eight months is a long time in the life of a two-year-old. We have both grown used to your absence in our lives. We shall continue like that! I cannot go back to the situation you put me into. I have had a long time to think about it.' With that she went back to sleep. The drug they had given her was too strong to resist.

When she awoke next, Sandro was not there, and she thought she must have had a bad dream. The nurse had woken her for the baby's feeding time.

'We sent your husband to the cafeteria for coffee. He needed something to keep him awake. He looked very tired. We understand that he has just arrived from Argentina. There is a parenting room available if you wish it.'

'You will have to ask him what he wants. I am not too happy with him at the moment!'

'Just because he missed the baby's birth? It is not always easy to predict when they are going to arrive. They have their own timetables, and this one is two days early. Babies are so unreliable!'

'Well, he had plenty of time', mumbled Bethany and changed the subject.

Shortly after, Sandro appeared again and asked her if she wanted to continue the conversation now or after he had a short sleep.

She abruptly said, 'There is nothing to say!'
He left her saying he would have a rest first. He had not slept for two days and did not want to get her upset while she was feeding the baby.

Bethany watched him leave and said to herself, 'If I was one day stronger from having the baby, I would pack the baby up and leave while he was asleep.'

Her tiredness overcame her, and she went back to sleep.

Awake again and she found Sandro by her bed again, looking a little rested. He started, 'Señor Lazar came to see me at the hotel a few days ago and said that you were enquiring about divorce proceedings. Bethany, I love you and do not want a divorce. I forgive you meeting with Miguel and giving him money. It is all over now!'

Bethany sat up straighter in her bed and exploded, 'You forgive me? For what, Sandro, am I being forgiven? For finding our son and rescuing him, or was it that I used my own discretion and my own money to show mercy to a small child who needed operations? Or bringing Maria and Matias to meet their grandchildren that they had never seen, and whose grandchild was in need?

Which of these things am I to be forgiven? And are your parents going to forgive me too?

No, Sandro, it is not me to be forgiven. It is not over yet! If that is your attitude, I do not want to be forgiven by you, because I do not think any of those things need for me to be sorry about. Yes, I will divorce you, and I do not think there is a judge in any country who will give you custody of your children under these circumstances. You have ignored Robert for eight months and he does not know you, and the baby is mine alone, because you have not once asked about how the pregnancy was proceeding and if she, or I were well. You cannot say you did not know I was pregnant because I was sitting opposite Señor Lazar when he advised you, and I also had the doctor who examined me to send you an advice, so you could not have overlooked it!'

She ran down at last, but everything had been bottled up so long she was not finished yet.

'I joined your family, aware of your personal need to tend your father. However, the wedding vows say that you should forsake all others and cleave unto your wife! I have taken third place in our life after your parents. You are the only thirty-year-old person I know that jump to your parents' commands! You shut Robert out of your life so that you could attend them. You left our house before he was awake in the mornings and went to your parents' house, and in the evenings, you arrived home from their house after he had gone to bed and he was asleep when you came to us. It took me a while to come to terms that you did not want your son, and I could not understand how you could ignore your own son, so that you focused on Miguel and not that your son was missing.

'I realised then what a mistake I had made. I thought all that time that I had a loving husband and family, and I was proved wrong, because I did not know the meaning of revenge and subservience! I have had a lot of time in the last eight months to think! I was trained as an hotelier! And you have shut me out of my hotel as well. Your reason was Robert was taking up all my time, and from the distance of Australia, I can see how much you have taken from me.

'You will have no choice now of buying me out of my share of the hotel when our divorce goes through. You will also have to add the amount of maintenance that you owe us for the last eight months and seeing that I am co-owner of the hotel I have not seen a statement for that length of time. This is something else a judge will not see in your favour that you have not played a part in the upkeep of your family for the last eight months!'

It was as if all the built-up bitterness came tumbling out.

She went on, 'I will ask my brother Mark to take you to our Shenton Park Hospital. It helps people without legs. Your father sat in his wheelchair all these years being waited on hand and foot by his wife, his mother, and his son when he could have been leading a busy life. It is only his legs that are paralysed. His mind and arms work perfectly well. He has sat brooding about Miguel and his bad luck all this time when he could have made a good life for himself.

'For instance, he could do the bookkeeping at the hotel. He has done the books for the ranch forever.

So, Sandro, I can see why an Argentine, beauty or not, had not married you. They would not have wanted to be the fly in the web spread out to catch them. It took a stupid Australian, who believed in love and fairness, to fall for you and into the web!'

For a long time, there was silence.

Sandro had not attempted to interrupt her and sat stunned by her attack. It occurred to her that probably no one had ever spoken to him like that before!

He stood up and stood silently by the window. He turned to her and asked, 'May I use your house while I am here? When you come home, perhaps we can have another conversation before I return to Buenos Aires. There is a lot I have to think about.'

She gave him the keys to her house and car, saying, 'My car is in the garage there for your use. Perhaps you can pick up Robert from my father's house so you can get to know each other again. He is a wonderful child and very bright, but do not get too close. Remember, Robert belongs to me. You have already abandoned him once, so if you don't want him, leave him at his grandfather's house. He knows they love him and is wanted there. I will be home the day after tomorrow.

My father will be picking us up to take to my house.'

Sandro looked close to tears as he left the room. 'Well,' she thought, 'he had asked for it!'

He did not come to the hospital the next day, and she was glad because she needed the rest before she went home the following day. The baby had been a little fretful, and she put it down to her unsettling day with Sandro. She had calmed down and felt much better after her big explosion. Her father picked her next day to ferry her home, and she asked him if he had seen Sandro.

'Yes, he came and delivered Robert to them to play with Mathew before going to Shenton Park with Mark, and then taken him home again when he returned. Sandro seemed very subdued when he had seen him. What did you say to him?'

'Eight months of frustration and anger, and he did not say a word.'
'Are you still thinking of divorcing him?'
'He has two days till he returns to Buenos Aires to think about all I have said to him, so I will wait and see what he replies to me. I didn't give him much chance to speak when we met. Is he at home waiting for me now?'

'Yes, he thought it better to stay with Robert to meet you in your home, but do not start arguing in front of Robert. Wait until he has gone to sleep. The poor child is still wary of Sandro.'

As the car stopped in the driveway of Bethany's town house, the front door of the house flew open and Robert spilled out of the house. 'Mummy, Mummy, Daddy is here! Where is my baby sister?'

He was so excited that Bethany and her father burst out laughing, and his granddad picked him up to show him the baby through the car window. 'Is she going to stay with us, Mummy?'

'Yes, the baby is all ours, Robert.'
Sandro came over to them and lifted the baby's capsule from the car, gazing at the baby girl in wonderment. 'Look, Robert, it is a real baby girl. See how pretty she is?'

Robert leaned over and with awe in his voice said, 'She is the smallest person I have ever seen.'

They all laughed and went into the house, including her father, as he still had not seen the baby properly yet.

They let Robert hold the baby in his lap, and he asked what her name was.
'Gina Sofia Rodrigos,' Bethany announced, 'for my two mothers. We shall call her Gina. Robert, can you say that?'

'Gina', he said. 'That is easy. Is it the same in Spanish?' looking at his father.
'Yes, Robert, names are the same in both English and Spanish. You speak both very well. Your mother is a good teacher.'

Her father then left them, saying, 'Come to dinner tomorrow night so that we can celebrate your birthday, Bethany, and Gina's too. Your grandparents will be there, and they have not met Sandro yet. Mathew is anxious to see the baby too.'

After he was gone, Bethany turned to Sandro and said, 'I have to feed the baby and then I must have some sleep. I am still drowsy from the medication I was given at the hospital. They thought I needed it to calm me down. Can you manage Robert for a while without me?'

'I will take him for a walk to the park to give you a quiet moment to feed Gina. They told me at the hospital that you need rest and quietness to concentrate on the baby while she is still so new', and taking Robert by the hand, they left her.

It was so quiet when they left – no voices, no clanging from trolleys and trays. It was heavenly quiet. She turned on the radio to find some lulling music and picked up Gina and fed her. After settling the baby, she snuggled into her own bed where the scent of Sandro hit her with nostalgia. How she had loved him! Could she love him again? She drifted off to sleep hearing Sandro and Robert tiptoeing in to look at her and at Gina.

When she awoke, she showered, and following the smell of cooking, she went to the kitchen and saw Sandro stirring something in a pot on the stove. She had never seen him cook before. He hadn't needed to cook, with his wife, mother, and grandmother ready to jump at his every need.

He turned when Robert said, 'Hello, Mummy, look at the new car Daddy has bought for me.'

Sandro saw her smiling and put down the spoon he was holding and moved to hold her to him. It felt so good. How she had missed him and his love! She started sobbing. She could not help herself. The sobbing just burst out from her, and she could not stop.

Sandro turned off the stove and picked her up and carried into the lounge room and sat down holding her and rocking her, with Robert following, very concerned.

'What is wrong with Mummy? Does she hurt?' he asked his father.
'Yes, my son, she hurts in her heart, but I hope she will be better soon. We will let her cry a bit and then we will kiss her better and have our dinner.'

Robert came closer and put his arms around Bethany too and said, 'Don't cry, Mummy. I love you. You do not need to cry anymore.'

Bethany started to laugh. 'Oh Robert, you have saved my life! See how I am better already because you love me!'

Sandro murmured, 'And I love you too, my darling. I think I have come to realise in the last few days just how much I love you, and I am sorry for what I have put you through.'

'Are you really, Sandro? You will have to prove it to me because the hurt of your absence in our lives runs very deep. I do not know now whether I can trust your words. I will need proof. I gave up my life here in Australia and my family and friends to put my trust in you, and you abandoned me and your son and daughter! It will need a lot of proof to win us back. I know I still love you, against my will, but there is more to love than sex and feelings. There is trust and caring, and I'm not sure I can trust you enough now to care enough for us to come back to you.'

'Give me a chance to prove it, Bethany. I will try very hard to make it up to you for what I have done.'

Robert said, 'If you are better now, Mummy, could we have our dinner? I am very hungry.'

'So am I, Robert,' Bethany and Sandro said together. Sandro got up to serve the stew he had made, which was surprisingly good despite his lack of experience as a cook.

They bathed Robert together and put him to bed. Sandro read him a book, and they kissed their son goodnight.

Robert said sleepily, 'It is good to have a daddy and a mummy, like Uncle Mathew' and fell fast asleep at once.

Bethany bathed Gina and fed her and at last came and sat with Sandro.

'I went with Mark yesterday to your orthopaedic hospital, and it has given me much to think about. We have such a hospital in Buenos Aires, but my father refused its attentions. He did not like strangers in his life. So, he refused the nurses we tried out for him, and I now realise how selfish he has been. From the age of sixteen I have been tending to him and took it for granted that it was my duty to look after him.

After seeing all the innovations for paraplegics that Mark has shown me, I can see I was blind to tradition and what was expected by me by my family. There is a method available to lift him in and out of his bed. He could have a specially innovated car to drive after using the special lift to lift him out of the wheelchair. You are right. There is nothing wrong with his arms or his mind. Hospital staff told me that it would take some time to retrain him in all that is available, although the hospital staff here also said that wanting to do it is the main factor.

'I shall move into the apartment as soon as I have discussed it with him. Then he will not have any choice but to have someone else. I think that was the message Señor Ortega was giving me when he left the apartment to me on our marriage, but I was so blind!

'Also, the hotel bookkeeping is a good idea of yours. It would not take him long each day, and it would give him an interest and some money to help with his orthopaedic apparatus.'

Bethany smiled 'I am glad you went with Mark. I was not sure you would go, but I see you have taken it to heart to change things. It will give you so much more time for yourself to concentrate on other things. I have another idea which you may consider too way-out for you. I am going to say it anyway, seeing as you are in a listening-to-me mode!

'I think you should go and see Miguel! It will settle your niggling feeling that I had something to do with Robert's kidnapping and that I found him because I knew where he was! I found him because one of our neighbour's nursemaids saw the kidnapping and recognised the woman with Miguel as being her mother's near neighbour, and led me to him. Maria will confirm this because she came as well. Miguel was struggling to support his family, and his eldest son was sick and unable to walk. I recognised the irony of this, of course, but when I saw the child lying on his bed unable to move, I gave him the money for the operations he required. It was as simple as that. He had treated Robert well, and Robert seemed to enjoy being with the other children and suffered no harm from it all and has no bad memories of it at all.

'Miguel appeared to me to be sorry for shooting your father and said when he came from the high from the drugs, he had taken that day, he was ashamed and had never taken drugs or alcohol since that day.'

Sandro went to say something, but Bethany stopped him. 'I have not finished yet. I must go on, as I may not have the opportunity again. Matias is growing older and unable to do all the things required and needs some help. I don't know if you have done anything about extra help yet for him, but why not ask Miguel to help him? Miguel was brought up on the ranch and knows the work. Miguel and his family could live in the cottage, and they could fix up the extra living quarters for Maria and Matias to retire to, and eventually Miguel could take over and a pension paid to Matias for all his years of work. The workers' quarters could be made nice for them at little cost. It would be nice for them to get to know their grandchildren better. It would solve a big problem coming up at the ranch, but first your parents would have to accept Miguel's apology face-to-face.'

Sandro stared at her, trying to understand all she had said to him. Then he smiled. 'I have always admired your business acumen, my love. As a business deal, this is certainly admirable, but I would have to talk very hard to my father to get him to agree to it. It is not my ranch yet, so I can be ignored on this, but I promise I will try. What else do you want me to do as proof? Do you want to live in the apartment at the hotel, or do you want a house of your own?'

' I want a house of my own with a garden and room to move. The children need a garden they can play safely in until they get a bit bigger, somewhere where it is safe.

' I do not want to see your parents unless we are invited to a special occasion or we invite them for a special occasion. I have learnt to hold a grudge! Something I have never done before or was even aware of in my life before! Something I have learnt from your family!

'You will have to go to the ranch with them each fortnight as you will eventually own the ranch and must keep up with its maintenance. The children and I will not fit into the car, as we will be required by law to have car seats for both children. Perhaps we can go alternate weekends as a family outing for the four of us. I did love the ranch when we went, but things have changed now.'

'Can we afford a house, Bethany?'
'I can afford a house, Sandro, and it would be in my name alone, so next time there is a marriage problem, you will have to be the one to move out.'

Sandro leaned over and took her hand. 'You have had it hard for the past eight months, but they have been the worst eight months of my life. It took me a while to see things from your point of view. Of course, I knew in my heart that you did not have anything to do with Miguel, but I was completely brainwashed by my father. I realise that we treated you badly, and I am thoroughly ashamed. I love you truly. I did not stop loving you, but habits of a lifetime are hard to break, and my parents influence was total. I love you, Bethany, and just want to be a family with you and the children and bring up our children together.'

'When are you returning to Buenos Aires, Sandro?'
'In three days time. Daniel is very confident that he can manage things. He is a good chap and can always ring if there is a problem. Do you want me to stay longer?'

'We shall wait until after my father's dinner party to decide. If you stay longer, the airline will take into account that you came for the birth of a child and will defer the departure for you. If I decide to go back to Buenos Aires, it would not be for at least one month, to get Gina settled into a routine before a long trip. That will give you time to sort things out at home. My grandparents, my mother's parents, will be at Dad's tonight to meet you and to welcome Gina for the first time. They already know Robert and love him.'

Chapter 10

The dinner party was a great success. Sandro turned on his charm for Bethany's grandparents, and they were impressed by his good looks and courteous manner.

Mark and Sandro had a long talk about paraplegic apparatus and got on well with each other.

Grandmother thanked Bethany for naming her baby 'Gina' after their daughter (a weepy moment). Robert was very happy, seated next to his young uncle Mathew, who thought the baby 'cute'. Jenny and Laura both had a nurse of the baby with smiles on their faces, maybe with thoughts of things to come.

Bethany looked at her father and saw a look of satisfaction on his face. All members of his family were present and happy.

He approached her later and asked, 'How is it going?'
'I think I may be going back to Buenos Aires!'
'On your conditions?'
'Yes, Dad, on my conditions! They are pretty stringent, but he has agreed so far. But I will not go for at least one month, to get Gina settled and for him to set up our new life together. If he does not, he knows I will not go.'

'Good girl, you know that we are in your corner, and we will back you up all the way if you decide to stay here or if you decide to go. We are here to help!'

She hugged her father. 'Thanks, Dad. I know you have always been in my corner, and that has kept me going since Mum died.' She paused.

'In a way, these eight months apart has been a huge learning curve for both Sandro and me. We married so quickly we did not have a chance to learn about each other and our differences in culture. I had been so happy I hadn't seen the catastrophe coming, but it will not catch me out again. I've taken care of that, and Sandro now understands it as well. We still love each other, Dad. I have never felt like I could love anyone else like I love him. He occupies my mind and heart even with the dents of the last eight months.'

'Why doesn't Sandro take some more time here? As far as I know, he hasn't had a break since your honeymoon at the ranch. He deserves a holiday and what better timing for it? You could take him on a tour of south-west of Western Australia and show him some of the self-contained cabins and chalets. It might put some ideas into his head for when he takes over the ranch.'

'It is a good idea, Dad. Would you and Jenny look after Robert for us? I have to take Gina because of feeding. Sandro has not spent much time out of Argentina. It may well be an eye-opener to him as Argentina was for me.'

'I am sure Jenny will not mind and just look at the boys together. I think they would be happy too.'

Bethany opened her birthday presents with her family after dinner, and Sandro watched her with her family and later said, 'I know now what I have taken you from. Your family has such a generous hold on you and did not try to hold you from what you want to do.'

He had felt so much love in the room when they were all together. How friendly they were to him even after he had treated her so badly!

'It is the Australian way, Sandro. Together we will find a path that is right for us for our children as they grow. Having you with me tonight made me so happy.'

'I am glad, Bethany, because I like your happy face much more than your angry one. I haven't seen you angry before, and it frightened me, knowing I had caused it.

I have a birthday present here for you', he said, taking out a gift-wrapped parcel from his pocket and handing it to her with a kiss. 'With all my love.'

She unwrapped it and drew out a diamond ring from the box.
'I did not give it to you at the dinner party because I thought you had a right of refusal if you did not want to wear it, and I did not want to embarrass us in front of your family.'

Bethany put her arms around him and kissed him.

'Sandro, I love you, and I guess I always will, because even when I was so angry with you, I still loved you. I would rather not get angry again. It does not feel right to me. I would rather be a happy person. You told me once I was the smiliest person you had ever known, and I want to return to that from now on. I will wear your ring.'

This time he kissed her, long and thorough.

She said, 'Out of curiosity, Sandro, what made you arrive when you did without warning?'

'When Señor Lazar came to my office at the hotel to tell me that you were enquiring about divorce proceedings, he casually mentioned that the baby was due this week, and it was also your birthday soon. It was said in such a casual way that it took me a few minutes to process it all after he had gone. I immediately booked an airline ticket and called Daniel in take over from me, then packed and left. I thought I would arrive in time for your birthday and be here when the baby arrived, but she came two days early to confuse things.'

'It is like the nurse said in the hospital. You can't always count on babies to come on time.'

After feeding the baby, they went to bed together, with Sandro holding her in his arms, knowing they could go no further so soon after the birth of the baby, smelling the sweetness of her, both feeling the contentment of being together.

The next day Sandro rang Daniel and told him he was staying another week. Bethany packed Robert's things and took him to her father's house. They then packed their own things and set off for the picturesque south of the state.

Bethany had booked on the Internet different type of accommodation for the next four nights to give Sandro a glimpse of what was available in the way of short-term stays.

They had a wonderful time together, visiting wineries. Sandro even tried surfing the waves at the beach near Margaret River, something he had never done before, with Bethany and the baby watching from the beach under a sunshade.

They tried all the seafood, so plentiful from the ocean and rivers, loving the yabbies, a small crustacean that was delicious, from the small farms along the way, and trying the fresh prawns and lobsters. One night's stay was at a farm where the farmer had a nursery of piglets, lambs, and goats. Robert would have loved helping the farmer collect the eggs from the chickens, so they would bring him next time they came.

Sandro was very impressed with all the stays and said that he could well imagine some of the cabins on the ranch. Bethany kept very quiet about it because it had to be his own idea if it was going to happen.

They returned to Perth, comfortable in being with each other again. The baby had not been any trouble.

They drove over the Swan River, sparkling under the bridges, past Kings Park with its wonderful views of the city and went to pick up Robert from her father's house. He hadn't missed them at all, because he had his uncle to play with for four whole days and nights! With two days to go before Sandro was to return to Buenos Aires, Bethany rang her university friends to make a date to meet for a drink. She had not contacted any of them whilst she was here alone, so now she thought they would like to meet Sandro, thinking they were there as a family from Argentina for a holiday. They took the children to be admired, of course. The women admired Sandro and the children, and the men talked about Argentina and were very interested.

Bethany was pleased that Sandro could see her in her own surroundings, not just in his, so he would have more insight into her previous way of life, which he seemed to be enjoying immensely. They drove back home to Bethany's town house via the ocean beaches and stopped to watch some surfers. They returned via the Swan River again and watched the yachts racing on the sunlit waters, without a cloud in the sky. It was a beautiful day and one that would stay in their memories forever.

****

The time came for Sandro to leave for Buenos Aires. They found it hard to part, but he had to go. Before he left, Bethany gave him a new iPhone so that he could speak face-to-face with Robert and to keep in touch with the children.

It was so quiet when he had gone, but she refused to cry in front of the children, so she packed them up and went to visit her grandparents, who were always happy to see her and the children.

Sandro phoned on FaceTime most days, bringing her up to date with his activities and talking to Robert. He went to see Miguel and got his OK to talk with his father. Bethany suggested that the interview take place at the ranch with Marias' pleading eyes that might influence his father.

He had moved out of the house into the apartment and was looking for a house, but nothing had come up yet.

He had made an appointment at the hospital for his father to attend and had a nurse to help until other arrangements could be made.

And then one Monday, Sandro reported that they had met Miguel at the ranch and Miguel had been forgiven. He would move into the house with Matias and Maria until the renovations were completed on the workers' quarters and his family could join him. The childs back had been operated on and had been successful, and he was learning to walk. Thanks to Bethany! She felt so exultant after that call! She hoped it would all work out.

Then Sandro reported that his father was interested in doing the bookkeeping for the hotel. Margarite, the lady who did it now, was quite happy to step down, as her daughter had just had a new baby and she wanted to spend some more time with her grandchildren.

Things were certainly happening. Then Sandro announced that he had found a suitable house. An old acquaintance had died suddenly and his widow wanted to sell her house and go and live with her daughter. She would wait for Bethany to come and see the house. He had been to see it, and it looked very nice.

It was an old house, as most of them were close to the hotel, but it had been kept in excellent condition and would make a nice family home. The gardens were extensive, and there was a small apartment at the back where the couple's housekeeper had lived, separate from the main house and near the laneway that ran down the rear of the property, so that anyone living there had no need to come near the main house to come and go. The gardens were so large that a gardener may be needed.

Do you remember Manuel, the odd-job man that had been working at the hotel for some time? He could live in the apartment with his wife. Manuel could do the gardening two days a week and his wife Anita could help in the house for those same days.

So, it was time for Bethany to go. She organised the airline tickets and packed up, said a weepy goodbye to her family, and set off for Argentina.

This time when she arrived at the Buenos Aires airport, she was holding the hand of her own child and carrying the baby girl and was welcomed by the same man holding a placard, this time with Señora Bethany Rodrigos written on and a big grin on his face as his sunshine lady came towards him.

Chapter 11

Bethany loved the house that Sandro had chosen for her. It was bought with most of the furniture in situ, because it fitted so well with the house. The house had been built in the early 1900s and had been in the same family since it was built and excellently maintained through the years.

She felt it had the same comfortable feeling as the ranch house. It had been a family home until recently.   The elderly lady was going to live with her daughter and did not need much from the house.

The gardens were extensive, with a small apartment towards the rear of the property, separate from the main house, and Sandro had organised Manuel and his wife Anita to move in.

Robert had taken to Manuel at once, following him around the garden. Manuel was a patient man, describing to Robert which were weeds that needed to be pulled out and which plants were to be watered. At the moment, they were digging a vegetable garden, Manuel with a big spade and Robert with a small one.

Anita was a round, rosy person with a ready smile, willing to do what was asked of her. Bethany felt that she could be a safe person to leave the children with, although she did not want to until they got to know each other better.

The Hotel Aria was thriving. The wedding venue was a huge success.Almost every Saturday evening was booked for some months ahead and deposits paid. Bethany suggested getting a liquor license so that they were able to serve drinks at the weddings. She also thought this would bring their occupancy rate up at the hotel for the rooms as more people would stay the night rather than drink and drive. This ultimately turned the occupancy rates to almost 100 per cent each Saturday night, with many of them staying on for other nights as well.

 Sandro's apartment too was a popular choice for bride and groom for the weekends, also sometimes longer.

Sandro was now contemplating using the carriage he had stored in the stables at the ranch to complement the wedding party journey around to the apartment.

He thought Manuel would like to do this as he had been a gaucho in his youth and knew how to manage horses. Betsy might still be up to pulling the carriage. She had been the horse to pull the carriage for Sandro's father before he got his special saddle. Betsy was getting old, so she would be docile. They should set the carriage up first to see if she was still capable of pulling it with three people in it, before they advertised it for the wedding parties as part of a promotion.

If Betsy was up to it, they would have to apply to have a horse stabled in their garden. There was plenty of room, and she would get used to Manuel feeding her, and the children would love having her there.

Sandro had continued his fortnightly visits to the ranch with his parents. One day he came home, quite perturbed, saying that his father had started to tell him stories from the past.

It seemed Maria, Matias' wife, had claimed she had a one-night stand with Tomas Rodrigos, who was Phillipe's brother, before Tomas disappeared. Maria had lived in the local town close to the ranch, and it had been Tomas' nineteenth birthday party, and Tomas had come home from Buenos Aires, where he went to university and sex had taken place that night at the party. Tomas had returned to the city next day and then disappeared a short time later.

Maria had come to the ranch and claimed she was pregnant with Tomas' child, and she was turned away by the Rodrigos family.

The next thing they knew about it was she married Matias Horta, who worked on the ranch for them.

At the time, Matias lived with his parents in the town, but on his marriage, he had applied to them to live in the cottage with his new wife Maria.

The Rodrigos were always wary of Maria, and they had never felt close to her as they were with Matias. Phillipe and Matias had gone to school together and were the best of friends.

The time came, though, when they thought that Maria had been encouraging their son Miguel to think of the ranch as his inheritance. This seems to fit in with the surly behaviour towards Phillipe when Phillipe told him what to do on the ranch and his general behaviour.

Phillipe also believed that Maria Horta knew all along where Miguel had gone, after shooting Phillipe, but had kept it quiet from Matias.

Phillipe had been quietly quizzing Matias in a roundabout way as to Maria's movements in the last few years. It seems that she caught the bus to the city to go shopping and stayed out all day, at least once a fortnight. Matias had not questioned her because it was a lonely life for a woman at the ranch all day while her husband was working for days on end. Phillipe believed that she was visiting Miguel and his family.

He also believed that it was Maria who orchestrated the kidnapping of Robert, involving Bethany, because she thought Bethany would be a softer touch compared to the rest of the family.

Since Miguel had been back at the ranch, Phillipe had ordered a DNA test done on some hairs he had found from the hat Miguel wore. The test had been done and showed Miguel was not a relation of the Rodrigos family. Miguel had been acting as if the ranch was his and questioning everything Phillipe and Sandro said. It was a big mistake to take Miguel back on the ranch. However, Phillipe was now saying that it was better to have your enemy close to you so you could find out their next moves.

Bethany was in shock! She had been outmanoeuvred by Maria! It was all her fault for suggesting Miguel go back to the ranch! It could be a big disaster, and Sandro could be the target next time!

She had not been to the ranch since returning to Buenos Aires. Moving into the house, taking care of the children, helping organise the wedding venue had taken up all of her time, and she made a decision now that she would not take Robert to the ranch while Miguel was there. They had to find a way to get Miguel off the ranch again.

The next time Sandro came from the ranch, he said that Matias was not well. He had been to the doctor, but they did not know what was wrong with him.

Sofia thought that he had been poisoned! He had stomach cramps, was very drowsy, and was hallucinating. The next day he was better, but these episodes went on, each one worse than the last one. Eventually, after three months he succumbed and died, still not diagnosed by the doctor.

Phillipe, Sofia, and Sandro visited the doctor and requested a post-mortem be done on Matias. The doctor agreed because he was unsure what Matias had been suffering from.

When the post-mortem was finished, the results showed that Matias had died from poisoning. There were distinct white spots on his kidneys consistent with a rare poison from a plant that Phillipe acknowledged grew on the property. It was usually a quick acting poison, but it must have been administered in small doses over a long period to give it the appearance of a rare disease. It was a cruel death given by a cruel and uncaring person!

Phillipe was so angry that his friend had died like this. He knew it was Maria or Miguel! He took the results to the police, but they said there was no proof that he had not taken it himself as a way-out. And they were far too busy to investigate.

Phillipe was so dejected he mourned his friend of so many years. He had known Matias most of his life. And he had been a true friend.

He ordered the work on the living quarters to stop and told Miguel to leave and take his mother with him! Miguel refused to go!

The Rodrigos family felt there was some sort of stand-off happening. They talked it over, and all decided that Maria had poisoned Matias because he had got in their way and to stop him interfering in the takeover of the ranch. They did not know what the next plan of the Hortas was going to be.

Sandro was torn between the ranch, the hotel, and the family he cared so much for and did not know what to do about Miguel.

Chapter 12

Meanwhile, Phillipe had his own plan!

Sofia and Phillipe had hired a taxi to take them to the ranch. He took his shotgun and went to the cottage and shot Maria dead. He sat in his wheelchair and waited in the cottage until Miguel came back and then shot him dead too. He then returned to the ranch house where Sofia waited and shot her and then shot himself. The housemaid who came in the morning found them all and notified the police.

Phillipe had left a letter, which was as follows:

'For the Authorities:
To conclude the death of Matias Horta, I enclose the autopsy report.
For the deaths of Maria and Miguel Horta. I hold them responsible for my friend Matias Horta's death. I also found them responsible for kidnapping my grandson and holding him for ransom.

This was the only way to conclude the stalking and continual harassment from an evil woman and the grandiose ideas she had for her son who participated with his mother to bring down the Rodrigos family.

'I have shot my wife Sofia at her request, and my own death also will complete the saga, so that life can go on without the continual danger that Maria and Miguel Horta held for the Rodrigos family.'

To Sandro he left a copy of this letter and deeds to the ranch and the town house. His will stated that his son Alessandro Rodrigos was now the owner of the ranch and town houses, along with all his worldly goods. He also left a goodbye letter stating that he had been feeling ill, and he had been advised by his doctor that his kidneys were failing. His general health was deteriorating, and both he and Sofia were happy to leave the world where Maria and Miguel had generated so much hate and caused such havoc that their world had stood still because of it.

Sandro cried when he read this. It had been hard on them all since leaving the ranch full time. He had not expected this! He did not know what to do. After the funerals and all the questioning from various Authorities, he talked it over with Bethany. She suggested that he ask advice from Phillipe's compatriots in the smoker's room at the hotel on Thursday night when they got together. They were all mostly experienced in the running of a ranch.

Thursday night he went to the smoker's room and told them what had happened to his family and explained that he was at a loss to know what to do, as he was still in shock. There was a general willingness to help. Phillipe had been one of them! They were all appalled at what the family had gone through because of a devious woman's greed.

They all agreed that, first of all, a new manager was necessary. One grand old gentleman said he knew of a young fellow who may be able to fill the position of manager. He was the brother of his own manager who was a great chap and an asset to his ranch, so his brother would come well recommended. He had never managed a ranch but had worked and lived on ranches all his life. Others offered bits of advice, which Sandro listened to and thanked them for. However, he thought the first gentleman's advice was the best. He made an appointment for Saturday morning in his hotel office.

Luis Fernandez came on time, dressed in black trousers and white shirt, accompanied by his wife Rosa.

When Bethany saw Rosa, she immediately hugged her and explained to Sandro that this was the nursemaid who had helped her at Robert's kidnapping rescue. Rosa explained that she had been working as nursemaid to fund her wedding to Luis at the time; they were married shortly after.

Luis turned out to be a personable young man, stating that he had not managed a ranch previously, but he was eager to have the chance to better himself and at least try it out. He was sure experience on ranches would carry him through. He could always ask his brother if a problem came up.

Sandro liked his attitude and agreed to take him on for a three-month trial. They could use the cottage on the property, which was in good order and had been thoroughly cleaned by a team sent out from the nearest town.

He told them that his family went to the ranch every second weekend to check on things and help out, but he would go each weekend for a month or until Luis felt confident that he knew what to do. There was a list of instructions nailed to the back of the laundry door of the cottage if required. This was probably all he needed because of his experience with horses and stock.

Luis was willing to start the next weekend. He had to give a week's notice where he was employed at the moment.

Bethany and Sandro felt quite happy that this problem was resolved, and they could trust their employees. They went overnight to check the readiness of the cottage for the new couple.

It was a bittersweet time for them. So many good times had been had there at the ranch and now some terrible ones that they were still dealing with.

The cottage was spotless. They fed the stock, checked the water, and turned down some fresh hay for the horses and were left feeling better than they had for some time.

The children were good, Robert following them around and helping and Gina sitting in her pram and smiling sweetly at everything.

Bethany felt good at the ranch, despite the terrible things that had happened there recently. It was a year since she had been there, but Betsy knew her right away, giving her a snicker when she approached her. Robert did not seem to worry at the size of the horses, giving them pats and rubs just as his father was doing. A good sign!

Back in the city, the nostalgia continued, and they agreed they would try to get there much oftener as a family.

Chapter 13

Sandro's grandmother, now a slightly unsteady eighty-five-year-old, had decided she would go into a retirement village, turning down Bethany's offer of a room at her house, stating that she was past young children and preferred her own age group nowadays.

So Sandro decided to rent out the town houses as self-contained holiday units through the hotel, and once again it was a great success.

He cleared out the family personal things from the units himself, including his father's stock books, ranch papers, and everything else he could find – photos and memorabilia, notes and letters and anything else that may be of importance to the future next generations, before letting in the cleaners to ready the units for rent.

The houses still looked like quality, and the furniture was in good condition, so he asked a premium price, and it seemed there were quite a lot of people willing to pay the price for them.

Three months of Luis' time at the ranch went fast, and he was taken on full time. He was an energetic young man, and things were looking good. The place had been in the doldrums for a while with just an aging man to look after things, so having a young energetic person around made a lot of difference.

Sandro was the one to mention self-contained units at the ranch. Things were going so well at the hotel that they could easily afford to build cabins at their ranch, like those he had visited in Western Australia with Bethany.

They discussed it with Bethany and Rosa, who both liked the idea of earning more cash for looking after them. The site would be chosen as soon as they had the quotes, and they would only build two at first, but they would look for a site where more could be constructed if the first ones did well. If they were not popular, he could use them for the hotel staff as incentive for service.

Bethany and Rosa would have a shopping trip in the city for the things required to furnish them. That sounded like fun!

Robert was now in kindergarten. He was an outgoing child and loved mixing with other children. At home Bethany was speaking to him in English. She had thought of asking Sandro to speak English to him as well as now he was away from home. Other people spoke Spanish to him, and she did not want him to lose his second language. It was such an advantage to be bilingual. Gina's vocabulary was 'Mama', 'Dada', and 'Wob'. That was as far as she had got. She seemed to get everything she wanted by just pointing and saying 'Ah'.

She was walking now. When she heard music, she would start swaying and wanted everyone else to dance with her, by holding up her arms, and usually got her way. She had blonde curly hair like Bethany and big brown eyes like Sandro, a lovely combination. Her disposition was sunny, finding fun in everything, and had everyone laughing with her. She was everyone's friend, especially Anita who loved her, and she became Anita's shadow around the house.

An unexpected visitor was shown into Sandro's office at the hotel one day – Terese Horta. The widow of Miguel stood before him. He gestured her to sit down. Sandro said nothing. He could not think of a thing to say. Terese had not been at home when he went to see Miguel.

Terese then said, 'Miguel's, Maria's, and Matias' belongings had been delivered to her house after the funerals. A wide-brimmed hat had been missing from the belonging. It belonged to my brother and loaned to Miguel when he went to the ranch, and now he wants it back. It was quite expensive and new, so he wants it returned.'

Sandro replied 'I asked for everything to be sent to you. I did not have an inventory. However, I will look around for it. It is possible that he left it in the stables when he returned his horse. I do not think the stables were searched at the time, so it is a possibility it may be there. I cannot guarantee it, as I do not recall having seen it there. If it is, I shall see that you get it.'

'Thank you'. Teresa answered politely and went on to say 'When Bethany was in the bedroom with my son and me while Robert was there at our house, Maria took swabs from Robert's mouth and from my children to send for DNA testing. The results have come back from the laboratory. They have only just come back as there had been a big backlog of work at the laboratory, and these had been issued as not urgent. We had expected them earlier, and Maria was upset that they had taken so long. The results show that the swabs were taken from the same family group!' She paused and took a big breath and said, 'Therefore, under the circumstances, I am now going to sue you for the ranch on behalf of my children!' She paused and went on, 'Because of your wife's mercy, my son is walking now after many operations on his back, so I will not ask for anything else. It will just be the ranch!'

She stood and handed Sandro a portfolio of papers, all very official looking. She said no more and walked from the room and the hotel.

Sandro went through the file. It was a fact!

His father had been right. It was what Maria had been waiting for. She had orchestrated things right from the beginning and had been waiting for the DNA results before the rest of the plan was executed.

And the hat! It had not been Miguel's after all, so the DNA results his father got could be wrong. He had cut off the serpent's head, but it had grown another one! There was still a battle for the ranch! Sandro rang the office of Señor Lazar the lawyer to make an appointment as soon as possible, and an appointment was made for the following day.

He then went home to his wife, his beloved Bethany, to tell her the sorry story.

They had loved the ranch so much, but it could belong to someone else soon! First of all, he had to cancel the home stays for the ranch as yet not started. Thank goodness! There was no use in building things to benefit Terese, the kidnapper of their son! He would tell Luis and Rosa as soon as possible; they may not want to work for Terese.

It brought up so many questions. Would the ranch house be included? He had an idea it was on a different title. Would the cattle and horses be included?

He must get all the paperwork he had brought from his father's house ready for the lawyer tomorrow. Whilst hunting through his father's papers, he came across some official papers pertaining to Miguel Horta shooting Phillipe Rodrigos. The police had accused Miguel of the crime and hunted without success, so it was not a closed case. He was not sure of the statute of limitations in a case like that, but it must be over if Miguel had come out of his hidey-hole.

He would take the papers to Señor Lazar to help him see the full affair, although he was sure that other than that there was not much value in them.

Bethany gave him the statement she had made with the lawyer after the kidnapping of Robert on his second birthday. He was astounded! He had not known she had done that. How incredibly stupid he had been at the time, treating her so badly! He would have to work harder on making her happy!

He examined the statement and all the photos she had taken of the Horta pair at the park, the white van at the park, and the white van outside of Miguel's house, Robert sitting on the floor with the other three children and a photo of the other boy lying on the bed with his mother beside him. She had also taken a photo of the money and the handing it over to Miguel. How clever she had been! And he felt quite tragic about not believing her at the time.

Also included was a photo of Maria and her grandchildren, the children from the passageway. He looked at it for some time. The photo showed that the children were familiar with Maria. One was sitting on her knee, another leaning up to her on her side. They were not strangers to each other!. Why hadn't he examined this statement and photos previously? He had not wanted to bring up a sad time with Bethany, and she had all the evidence of Maria's deception all the time, and he had ignored it, looking for an easy way out and now it had come back to it.

He went on thinking of the problems and Maria's part in it. He could see his father was right about Maria visiting Miguel; Bethany's statement confirmed it. The fact that Maria had taken Robert's DNA without permission must be illegal, and the extortion of the money was also illegal. He should have gone to the police with this information, and his mother and father might still be with them.

This made him feel dreadful and downhearted, blaming himself for all the things that had gone wrong. He pulled himself together, thinking it is too late to change some things, but he would try harder in the future.

Next morning , he laid out all the paperwork he could find for Señor Lazar, including Terese's folio of papers, Matias' autopsy, and his father's letter to the authorities and requested the lawyer to take up the case for them, if he was able.

The lawyer listened to him and agreed it was a complicated case, but worth battling. They had a good case for the shooting and the kidnapping that had taken place and good proof for that.

Also, Rosa and her mother as witnesses close to hand was a plus. The lawyer went on, 'The first thing to do is get another DNA test done with Sandro and the Horta children. That would save Robert having to attend. If it is done in a clinic, it cannot be faked. He would arrange a court order for the children to attend with their mother.

A valuation of the ranch should be done by a licensed valuer, and they would search the deeds of the property to see if other claims had been made and how they were satisfied.'

Sandro remembered that the property had been much larger in the long past. His father had told him that it had been broken up bit by bit to hand to second sons of the family, bits large enough to live on, with the main ranch going to the eldest son. He had not researched it because he had been too busy with his father's care and the ranch and hotel and now his own family.

Both he and Bethany loved the ranch and thought it worth battling for.

Señor Lazar warned them that it could be expensive, especially if it went to court. They insisted that they wanted to do it!

They shook hands with the lawyer and went home, dazed, but feeling they were doing the right thing under the circumstances.

Bethany remembered how Maria had fooled her. She had fallen right into Maria's deception and had been absolutely taken in at the time. How lucky that she had taken photographs of them all without Maria or Miguel suspecting! After remembering Robert playing with the Horta children in the passageway, she could not recall noticing any resemblance between them. She looked again at the photos that she had printed out. They looked nothing alike! The Horta children were quite small, as was Miguel. He was short and stocky and had hazel green eyes. He looked nothing like a Rodrigos. Bethany remembered Sandro saying how alike Ana's children were and so was Robert, the image of his father and grandfather, and even Gina had the brown eyes, although her hair was fair.

The DNA tests must have been faked surely. If it was Maria's doing, it was faked! She must have taken more swabs from Robert and sent them in as all the children!

Thank goodness for Señor Lazar! He makes you feel better even though things are bleak! He seemed to see straight to the basic details.

Bethany went all through the photos Sandro brought from his parents' house, looking for a picture of Tomas, but found none. Where else could she look? She mused, 'Of course, Grandmother would have photographs of Tomas. Mothers always had photos of their children, especially if they are deceased.'

She rushed to tell Sandro, who was looking through another box of memorabilia. They decided to ask her for lunch and ask her to bring the family photographs from before the 'dirty war' of the 1970s and Tomas' disappearance.

She did not know yet of the threat to the ranch yet, so it would be a good time to bring her up to date.

They thought it a good idea if Señor Lazar was there as well, if he could make it. His quiet questioning always helped bring out more from people, and Grandmother may know something about Maria's claim that Miguel was a Rodrigos.

So, she rang Grandmother and Señor Lazar to come to lunch for discussions on Friday.

Bethany organised the lunch. Anita was to serve it, leaving Bethany free to hear and see all that was going on and not miss out on anything.

Sandro's grandmother was an upright older lady with short wavy white hair brushed back from her face. It had a natural wave and was very attractive. She dressed in clothes that were a little old-fashioned but did not look wrong on her. She had an autocratic appearance, and her age carried it off well. She came in carrying a suitcase full of photographs.

They each looked eagerly at the photos but could find nothing or nobody that looked like Miguel, until Bethany picked up the photograph showing Tomas' graduation year from high school.

It showed a big group of teenagers from the town high school, with Tomas at the back, because of his height and down on the second row from the front. There was a boy who looked just like Miguel!

He was short and stocky and had straight hair, but they could not determine the colour of his eyes. On the back of the photograph were the names and signatures of all the students and clearly in a strong hand it read Enrique Gonzalez in the second row from the front!

'Bingo!' exclaimed Bethany, and the others turned and looked at her with smiles and looked at her find.

'Yes,' stated Señor Lazar, 'I think we have solved half the mystery, but how did Tomas get mixed up with Maria in the other half?'

The photo awakened memories for Grandmother Rodrigos. She explained, 'Yes, I remember that boy. He was Tomas' friend through school, and they went everywhere together until Tomas was sent off to university.'

Señor Lazar asked her, 'Was it usual for the Rodrigos boys to be sent off to university?' He thought most boys going to work on ranches went to agricultural college, especially if they were going to take over a ranch.

Grandmother answered, 'It was never intended for Tomas to take over the ranch. He had asthma from the time he was a small child. He had bad reactions from pollens and hay. We had decided from the time he was seven or eight that he should live in the city and learn another skill. We would purchase a business for him of his choice to compensate him for the loss of the ranch. Phillipe was much more sturdy, so the ranch would go to him.'

The lawyer asked about Maria's claim that Tomas had made her pregnant.
'Impossible!' she exclaimed. 'The night she claimed that Tomas had made her pregnant was Tomas' nineteenth birthday. He came home from the city to celebrate at dinner with us and was going to a party with his friends after dinner. It was a windy day in spring, and soon after his arrival, he was wheezing badly. By eight o'clock he was so bad trying to catch his breath that we asked Doctor Donati from town to come and help us. He stayed with Tomas for several hours, putting him into an oxygen tent. Tomas was in no state to go to a party and have sex with an unknown girl, believe me! We took Tomas back to the city early next morning, thinking we were saving his life! Only to lose him shortly after in the "Dirty War".'

'Is Dr Donati still alive?' queried the lawyer.
'Yes, I saw him at the theatre about six weeks ago. He came over to express sympathy for the loss of Sofia and Phillipe. He lives now in the city, but I do not know his address.'

'I will put my clerks on to looking for him. They can find a needle in a haystack when they really try. This could be the best way yet of defeating the Horta case. Would you mind, señora, if we make a deposition for you to sign stating what you have told us? For the claim against Señora Horta?'

'Of course, señor. Also, my nephew, my brother's son, is a judge. Do you think he could help at all?'

'What is his name, señora?'
'Rafael Mendoza. He is here in Buenos Aires.'

'Perhaps you could have a few words to him in private. One point, though – did you have any prior knowledge of what Phillipe was going to do?'

'Yes, we discussed it at length before he and Sofia went to the ranch that day. I tried hard to talk him out of it, but he was a stubborn man. He explained that his kidneys were failing him very fast and that he would be spending the rest of his life on dialysis. He could not contemplate that. He went once and came home so despondent. I also asked him, "Why Sofia too?" and she answered for herself, that without Phillipe there was no life for her.'

'Do not tell your nephew that you had prior knowledge of it. It could be construed that you were part of it, and for that you could be prosecuted.'

She gave him a startled look. 'By just knowing?'

'Yes, you should have advised someone, so they could have stopped it.'
'My goodness, I will be careful what I say. I did not realise. But there was no stopping Phillipe. I did try. He was my son, after all, and it is hard to lose sons, first Tomas and now Phillipe, and here am I, still going strong.'

Sandro went and hugged her. 'You are not alone, Grandmother. We love you, and we are here for you whenever we are needed.'

'Thank you, Sandro. I castigated your parents when Bethany and Robert left Argentina. I just could not get through to them that what they were doing was wrong. Your father was a very strong-minded man and thought he knew everything, but he was wrong. His hatred of Miguel and what he had done to him was so strong that he could not see that he was hurting others. His hatred of Maria and Miguel overcame his reasoning, and that was especially strong after what happened to Matias. Matias should not have died like that! When he allowed Miguel back on the ranch, it was to help Matias, not kill him!

Your father was devastated that he had lost his friend in such a way, and from that moment he had made up his mind what he was going to do.'

Señor Lazar turned to Sandro and asked, 'Do you think it better if I sit in with your grandmother's meeting with Judge Mendoza?'

'Yes, please, señor. I would hate anything to happen to Grandmother because of a stray word here or there by mistake.'

'Meanwhile, I will have my clerk search for Doctor Donati and also the man in the photograph. We will have the doctor give a statement if possible. At this stage, we will not try to interview the other chap until we have more. We do not want him to run away. Could you try and contact Judge Mendoza now, señora? I have my appointment book with me here, so perhaps we can tie up a time and date?'

She started to dial a number, but her hands were shaking, so she handed the phone to Sandro to dial it for her, which he did and handed the phone back to her to speak.

The judge listened to her as she told the story, and he seemed quite interested. He said he would have to see if he was allocated the case, as he would have to take himself off it because it was family, but he would like to help if he was able. He would have to get back to her as soon as possible when he had cleared his timetable.

Bethany laughed. She had not contributed much to the conversation to date. They all looked at her, and she explained, 'Señora Sofia had always said that Grandmother knew a lot of officials. What a godsend you are, Grandmother Rodrigos!' She added, 'Grandmother, would you like to go home and rest now? Or would you like to stay for a few minutes to see your great-grandchildren? They will be home any minute now. Manuel and Anita have gone to pick them up from the kindergarten and playgroup.'

As she finished speaking, the children came running into the house – Robert first, with Gina following after him. Robert ran straight to his great-grandmother and kissed her, Gina copying but obviously not knowing why. She had not seen the old lady as often, but Robert seemed to have memories from his earlier years when he had been quite close to her.

She was delighted. It had been her choice to go into a retirement village, but she had missed seeing the children. Robert had been a great favourite with her before he had gone to Australia with Bethany. Seeing how much they had grown, Robert so much like Sandro and Gina like Bethany but with Sandro's eyes, made her aware what she had missed out on.

Bethany could see all this crossing Grandmother's face and said gently, 'The children would like to see you more often than they do now. Because my family is in Australia, you are the only family we have here now. Sandro and I would also like to see you more often. Family is who you turn to in a crisis and who you celebrate with when there is a special occasion and have reason to celebrate. We have all missed you from our family scene, Grandmother Rodrigos.'

The old lady had tears in her eyes and said, 'Thank you, Bethany! I felt in the early days of knowing you that the lack of communication between us because of the language difference was a barrier to knowing you and felt you were uncomfortable with me. I can see now that you have made a family that I am proud to be a part of!'

She was looking so tired by now that Señor Lazar offered to drive her to her home, and she gratefully accepted, promising to come back soon.

Several days went past before Señor Lazar contacted them again to tell them he had contacted Doctor Donati, who confirmed that Tomas had a severe asthma attack on his nineteenth birthday. He had looked after him well into the night because of his extreme wheezing from lack of breath and had put him an oxygen tent, and he was unable to move. He had made a written statement to that effect.

The chap in the school photograph had been researched. He was still living in the same house, in the same town. He had been married but lost his wife to an illness. His only son lived with him and was unmarried. His son worked in the bakery with him that Enrique had inherited from his father.

A clinic appointment had been made for Sandro and the Horta children, although there was no guarantee they would have results quickly, unless they asked Judge Mendoza to intervene on their behalf. The judge had not got back to him yet, obviously because he was very busy.

Sandro noted the clinic appointment and thanked the lawyer for the update. He asked if there was any point in him speaking to Enrique Gonzalez would help in any way. He did not appear to be the sort of person who would disappear as he had been a long-time resident of the town.

The lawyers answer was 'If we had definite DNA evidence, it would be safer to confront him. Otherwise he would only deny it, and that would be the end of it. It is always better to have evidence before confronting anyone.'

He went on, 'We have a valuer visiting the ranch on Monday next week. Do you want to be there? It makes things easier if the owner is present to point out the boundaries for them. Otherwise, a lot of time is taken up measuring.'

'Yes, please, señor. It would be interesting finding out how much the ranch is worth. We have no idea of its monetary value. Till now it has never crossed our minds. It has just been "Our ranch" and always has been, and we love it for itself, not its value. That sounds naive I know, but my family have worked that land for many, many years. I mean, really worked it, because Matias Horta was the first manager ever, after his son Miguel shot my father. The only reason that I am not working it full time is that my father required care, which I have been part of since then, and now we have a hotel as part of our life as well. The ranch was my first home, and I love it and would not like to lose it. We go there to get refreshed after a busy week in the city, and it works every time. We hope that we can pass it down to our children as it has been done for a very long time.'

'I can understand that. Try not to worry too much. Until we have the DNA results, nothing much can be done, so enjoy your ranch for now.'

Sandro and Bethany decided to go to the ranch that weekend. Yes, they would enjoy the ranch again. The staff at the hotel were good at managing the wedding parties now and could be trusted to manage without their supervision. They had taken on Daniel's cousin Felix as assistant manager, and he and Daniel were taking it in turns to do the weddings and making a good job of it.

Señor Lazar had his hands on everything to do with the Horta affair as they now called it, so they did not need to worry. The valuer was coming to the ranch on Monday, so they had an extra day to enjoy the peace and quiet of the ranch together.

The children were looking forward to it. Robert was so excited that he would see the horses again. This time his father had promised he could ride one. Gina too wanted to ride a horse. Anything that Robert wanted, Gina wanted as well. They left as soon as the children came home from the care groups.

Bethany calculated that they would go to sleep as soon as the car started and wake up when they arrived at the ranch. They were always tired when they came home from care and kindergarten.

She could remember her trips to her grandparents' farm and saying, 'Are we there yet?' knowing full well that they were not but teasing her father.

It turned out she was right. The children woke when they slowed to open the gates, refreshed from their sleep and ready to go exploring.

Sandro had rung Luis to tell him of his arrival and to ask him and Rosa for dinner, so they could discuss things when the children had gone to bed and all was quiet.

Whilst Bethany organised dinner, Sandro took the children to show them around, especially the horses at Robert's request. He promised the children a riding lesson the next morning, but meanwhile they could get friendly with the horses by feeding them and patting them.

They came back into the house, flushed with pleasure and quite grubby. So they were quickly bathed and fed and put into beds – Robert in Sandro's old room and Gina in Ana's room.

Bethany and Sandro would now sleep in the room they had shared for their honeymoon. What memories it brought back to them!

Dinner was ready for their guests, and when they were seated, Sandro went through the 'saga', as he called it, starting from the beginning to up to date. He told them that he wanted them to hear straight from him, because there were often distorted stories that people had added on to.

Rosa knew some of the story, of course, but was staggered at the rest of it and its consequences so far.

They came to the possibility of a takeover of the ranch, but all agreed to wait and see the outcome before making any decisions. Luis said he was sorry for it all. He was so happy working on the ranch, and he and Rosa had been looking forward to bringing up a family there; it was such a good location. And such a lovely place to live.

Sandro was pleased with Luis' comments and said, 'Our lawyer and we are sure it is all a mistake. Maria had fooled her daughter-in-law too. Our lawyer is very good and is following up everything he can. However, if it does go to court, it would be a jury deciding on the outcome. They may feel sorry for Terese Horta having to bring up her children alone and make a decision in her favour. We are trying to stop it going that far, so cross your fingers for us!

'It also means that we will not be able to go on with the farm stay cabins. Until it is resolved, we have lawyers to pay. If we have to go to court, we have been warned it is very expensive, so we shall have to shelve the cabin idea for the time being.

'Also ,we have a valuer coming in Monday. We shall stay until they have finished. They will be looking over the property to give the court some idea of what Señora Horta is claiming from us.

To us it is an inheritance that means many generations of our family's work, and it would be a shame to lose it to someone we do not consider part of our family.'

They said goodnight to their visitors and checked their children on their way to bed.

Next morning the children were up early, clamouring to go on the horses, jumping up and down in excitement. Sandro laughed at them. What a sunny pair they were! And the excitement was catchy. Sandro felt the excitement too that he could teach them.

First, he took Robert on his horse in front of him, after making sure that Gina was sitting far enough away so she did not get trampled, showed Robert how to handle the reins and talk quietly to the horse as he went. After a several minutes doing this, he allowed Robert to try it for himself. He took Gina up in front of him on Betsy and went slowly. Robert was in heaven.

He loved every minute of it. Gina was happy to sit in front of her father. She was far too young to try it alone yet.Betsy seemed to know what was happening and went slowly without jolting.

When Bethany came out to call them for breakfast, she found three contented people. She looked at them for a while and decided the first thing she would be doing when she got back to the city was to purchase two child-size helmets, as it looked like it was going to be a regular thing, for a while anyway.

From that day, Robert went out on a horse alongside of his father, to check the fences, check the water and the stock, although the latter had to be done from a distance. It was far too early for trying to gallop. That would be practised at a later date when he was more experienced.

Robert even liked rubbing the horses down after their ride; anything to do with horses was to his liking. Sandro stressed that he was never to come into the stables alone. The horses were quiet for Sandro, but they might not like a small boy underfoot. Robert promised with earnest look in his eyes.   After Gina's first ride, she was happy to stay with Bethany, playing quietly or chatting, or reading a book together. Bethany still went out on Betsy with Gina in front of her for the early-morning rides. They went slowly, and the 'boys' went faster and further.

During these rides Bethany wondered if Grandmother might like to come to the ranch with them. She had lived for many years on the ranch before Phillipe took over from his father. She would enjoy watching Robert riding with his father, as she must have watched her sons with their father.

Perhaps she would enjoy taking Gina for walks or reading to her. She determined to ask her next time they met.

Chapter 14

Monday arrived with the valuer expected. The arrival at 10 a.m. included the valuer, his assistant, and Señor Lazar and all the equipment required for surveying.

Señor Lazar apologised for his unexpected appearance, saying he was curious to see Sandro in place at the ranch. So far he had only seen him dressed as a manager of a hotel. Everyone laughed, and it started the day off well.

They were welcomed with coffee and cake and then they went out with broad-brimmed hats to explore with Sandro.

They came back for lunch, and this time when they went out to finish the job, Señor Lazar stayed at the homestead with Bethany and the children.

Bethany said, 'I am glad you came, señor. We wanted to ask you but thought you may be too busy.'

He replied, 'I am glad I came. Sandro's love of the place infused me with curiosity to see it for myself, and now I am here. I can see why he loves it. It is a very peaceful spot and has its own beauty.'

Bethany said, 'The children love it too, perhaps for the novelty of it, as I have not brought them here because of the dramas and trauma that has taken place here recently. This weekend has been wondrous for them. Robert has had his first riding lesson and is already riding well. It is natural to him, and he has fallen in love with the horses.'

'I thought that seeing as we were in the area of the town where Enrique Gonzalez lived and worked, we might call into the bakery on the way back to the city to buy some bread. I might just have my phone in my hand, and if the opportunity came up, I might just take a photo of whoever serves me, or whoever is in the shop. My source tells me that they do not have outside help, so it would be either the father or the son, and if we are lucky, both of them.'

Bethany's eyes brightened. 'I had thought of doing that myself, but I am not the actress Maria was. It would look a little suspicious if I went in there, as I have never been yet. We bring all our provisions from the city. We do not stay long enough generally to go grocery shopping locally to buy extra provisions. They would be wondering why I suddenly needed bread when we have never need it before, and I would mess everything up.'

She went on, 'We did speak to our manager last night. His wife Rosa is the nursemaid that helped me the day we rescued Robert after his kidnapping. She led me to Miguel's house, you recall! They are on our side, if needed. Have you heard from Judge Mendoza yet?'

'His secretary rang me on Friday, to say he will be available next Friday. Would you be willing to host another luncheon on Friday next? There would be the same guests, and including the judge. Would that be OK? I thought it wonderful that the relaxed atmosphere brought out all of Señora Rodrigos' memory of those earlier years. It was pure gold!

'It would be good for the judge to hear first-hand the rest of the story from Sandro rather from me. He will then get the feeling of the trauma you have all gone through. If he gets the feeling that the terrible story has traumatised all of you, he may intervene in the case on your behalf. Before it goes to court, which is a very expensive experience. The jury may look at the case of Señora Horta losing her husband, the children's father and their grandparents, and may find in favour of them', he paused. 'I am looking at the worst-case scenario here, but strange things have happened in the name of the law! We must stop it going to court if we can!'

'Señor, you think just like my father. It must be international lawyers speak. He calms me down with a few words, and so do you. Do you have a family, señor?'

'No, sadly, I have been married to the law. I was so busy establishing my law firm that time went quickly and I left it too late to find a wife. I did not miss it when I was younger, but sometimes feel regret that I allowed time to pass by without having someone to share things with. I look at Robert and Gina and the regret hurts that I have left things too late.'

Bethany said, 'My father started in criminal law, which he always said excited him. The hours were long, so when my mother died, he changed to business law so that he could spend more time with my brother and me. We have appreciated him. He is a wonderful and loving father, and I do miss him. I have been having trouble sleeping for a while now and have tried to channel him, but haven't got through yet. This sort of thing makes you homesick for someone to talk things over with. Otherwise I am quite happy here.'

'Why are you not sleeping, Bethany? Is it because of the possibility of losing the ranch?'

'That is part of it. I have been having nightmares about the way Sandro's parents died. I have the dreaded feeling it was all my fault, because I was the one instrumental in getting Miguel back to the ranch. Maria read me like a book. I was so in love with Sandro and our son, I allowed her to manipulate me and I didn't see it. I even thought she was a nice person! Everything I have done for Sandro has backfired, and I feel I am a millstone around his neck! I have caused everything that has gone wrong! In the night when I wake up, I think he would be better off without me!'

'I have noticed that you do not have as much energy as before. How often do the nightmares come?'

'Several times a week now. I am exhausted most days. I try to hide it from Sandro. He has enough to worry about without this. He is too busy to have noticed that I am not myself.'

'I am positive that Sandro does not blame you now for anything that has happened. It is all in your mind, and you need a break from the scene to recover. Why don't you have a holiday in Australia with your father? You say he calms you down. If you have a break, you will see it more in perspective. You should stay until this ranch business is over. Sandro needn't know about the nightmares for now. He has so much on his mind at the moment. We do not want to add to his problems.'

'Your advice is always good, señor. I will think it over and talk about it to Sandro to get his opinion, not mentioning the nightmares. I cannot just say I am going without his approval. He may think I am abandoning him again.'

'Your health comes first, Bethany, so do not delay too long. It is a while since you returned to Argentina. You are looking after the children, handling traumas, looking after a house, a ranch, and helping at the hotel. This is a tremendous load for one person to carry. If the nightmares continue, you may collapse, and the way back to recovery would not be quick. That would not be good for you, Sandro, or the children! They all need you!

'Why don't you talk it over with Sandro's grandmother? She seems to have her head on right and sees things clearly. She has not gone into a mental decline like so many of her age. Despite the many traumas in her life, she seems to have come through quite well. She would understand the family feelings. Sandro took over his father's care at such a young age. It is a credit to him that he has survived so thoughtful and steady. The credit goes to you for his continued steadiness after his parents' deaths. Some people may have fallen apart at the way it happened, but because Sandro had you at his side, he has come through quite well. So, do not dismiss yourself as a millstone around his neck. The way I see it, you have been the one that has helped him through.'

He paused for a moment and then went on, 'This ranch business is a nuisance and should have never had happened. It is just a continuance of Maria's madness. Judge Mendoza will see it as such I am sure and will do his best to have the claim dismissed. You have both been too close to see it as madness, but that is what it is. Have a doctor give you an antidepressant. Sandro needs you right now until the case is over. Do you think you can manage till then? Then go off together to Australia away from everything that has happened, and I am sure the change of scene will do you both the world of good!

'This a third person's point of view of the whole story. It would have happened whether you were here or not. I think your father-in-law recognised this. That is why he went to the lengths he did to stop it. However, Maria had passed it down to her daughter-in-law before his death. She made plans that included you, because you were here. Even if you had not been, it would have happened in a different way. She had been intent with revenge for many years, no matter how mistaken it was, and it became an obsession with her and then with Miguel too.

Phillipe had half a lifetime to think about it from his wheelchair, and it was always going to happen one way or another. You cannot blame yourself for this! It was set in stone between them long before you came to Argentina.

'There! I have finished my summation to the jury, a bit long-winded but all true. I want to help you, Bethany. You are my favourite client, and I am pleased you think of me in a fatherly way. I would have loved to have a daughter just like you.'

'Thank you, señor. You have certainly summed things up for me. You are right about being too close to things. It does get you down. We got through Sandro's parents' deaths. It was appalling and so hard for Sandro. They had been so close for so many years. But then Terese Horta turned up, and it began all over again. How much can we stand?! Sandro is actually managing better than me, because he has the hotel to take his mind off things for a while, whereas I am home alone some of the time and churn things over.

'I will ask a doctor to prescribe an antidepressant. I will even take a sleeping pill at night, although I find those pills make me drowsy all next day as well, and I don't like that. I will try to wait things out and think only good things until this ranch business is over, whichever way it falls. I will talk Sandro into visiting Paris to see his sister and go on to Australia to see my family.

'You have made me feel so much better, señor. Thank you for making me see it all so much clearer than what I had in my head. I would be happy to be a surrogate daughter to you. You have the same calming effect as my father has. You must visit with us oftener so that you get to know Robert and Gina and they get to know you. I am sure Robert will recognise my father in you, and he loves his grandfather, so he will be happy to accept you as a surrogate grandfather.'

'Thank you, Bethany. I look forward to a long friendship!'
Just then the valuer and party came in. Bethany and Señor Lazar looked at each other. What such good timing! She made them a cold drink. They did not want coffee, and she gave them a pack of sandwiches to eat on the way home, via the bakery, and waved them goodbye.

Sandro suggested to Bethany that they stay the night at the ranch, as it was getting late and everyone was tired out, especially him, but he had enjoyed the day.

Bethany quizzed him on what the valuer had come up with, but apparently it would be a few days before they found out, as some research had to be gone into it and they may have an answer by Friday.

Bethany told Sandro about the luncheon with Judge Mendoza on Friday, with Grandmother and Señor Lazar, which she was going to organise again at their home, explaining that the lawyer thought it was a more congenial atmosphere when everyone relaxed and that he had thought Grandmother's contribution was 'pure gold' at the last meeting.

They bathed and fed the children and put them to bed. The fresh air at the ranch seemed to tire them out earlier. They sat out under the pergola with a glass of wine. Bethany felt as if a hammer had been lifted from her head. The blackness had gone, thanks to Señor Lazar! She did not mention the nightmares and headaches to Sandro but brought up the idea of a holiday to him, saying, 'Robert will be starting school next year, and in her experience school holidays were not a good time to travel, if you can avoid it. It would be best if they went on their holiday befor Robert started school'

She mentioned including a trip to Paris to see Ana and her family and saw his eyes light up.

She felt like saying 'Bingo' but held back. It seems a trip to Paris had been a dream of Sandro's for some time. It was a long time since his sister had left Argentina. It would be lovely to see her again and meet her husband and children.

Bethany was glad she had mentioned it and said, 'I would like to travel to Western Australia to visit my family. Perhaps we can go to Paris first and then go on to Australia. It is a long way, but we will live in these out-of-the-way places!'

Sandro laughed. It was as if the mention of a trip to Paris had picked him up, and he had something to look forward to.

They went off to bed together with their arms around each other, happy in each other's company as they had been before all the upheavals began.

Chapter 15

They went back to the city on Tuesday morning, refreshed and determined not to worry about the ranch until Friday.

Sandro attended the clinic with the Horta children and came home more than ever inclined to deny them as Rodrigos because of their looks. They all looked like Miguel, and not one of them had any Rodrigos features.

Friday came and Bethany once again had organised Anita to serve the meal and pick up the children, as she had done the previous time.

Sandro collected his grandmother from her home, and Señor Lazar arrived with Judge Mendoza. Everyone enjoyed the lunch. Bethany had become a good cook, coaxed by Señora Sofia in the early days of her marriage to Sandro to learn the dishes he liked best.

After lunch they moved to the lounge room, where Sandro started the story for Judge Mendoza.

From the beginning, with Maria coming in to say she was pregnant with Tomas' child – he went step by step, describing how it had all played out – up to the present case with Terese Horta.

The judge was a good listener. He clarified a few points along the way, especially Terese's part in the kidnapping of Robert, but otherwise silent until Sandro had finished the story.

He was quiet for a while, digesting it all, and then said, 'I have wonderful memories of your ranch when I was growing up. My parents took us there to visit my aunt and uncle several times a year until Tomas' disappearance. My brother and I were much the same age as Tomas and Phillipe, and we had marvellous days at the ranch, kicking a football, riding the horses, and I remember Tomas' propensity for asthma. We kicked up dust playing outside until he had to retire to his ventilator. Kids are cruel. It did not stop us playing polo or kick the football when he could not join in.

'We were all devastated when Tomas disappeared. My father was also a judge, a junior one at that time, and he went from place to place trying to find Tomas, or at least get some information, until he was warned that if he did not stop kicking up a fuss, his family could disappear too. In those days of the 'Dirty War', no one was safe. The only thing I can see to clear things up once and for all are the DNA results. Everything else is in your favour. I know someone at the clinic you went to this week. I play golf with him, so I will phone him now and see if he could hurry the results.'

He dialled his office and spoke to his secretary, and she gave him a number at the clinic to call, which he rang. After speaking for a few minutes to someone, obviously an old friend, he hung up, looking satisfied. 'Yes,' he said, 'we shall know early next week. My friend has ordered it to be done on Monday.'

'Hurrah!' they all sang out. Not one person in that room believed the former results had been genuine.

The judge spoke again. 'We could charge Terese Horta with kidnapping and extortion of $300,000 US. It is not a small sum.' He looked at Bethany as he said it.

She replied, 'If the DNA results go in our favour, I am willing to forget that. However, if they are Rodrigos, I would like to charge her. It was a very traumatic experience for me!

'As for the ranch, we are not willing to give it up! Perhaps she could be awarded a sum of money, minus the $300,000 US she has already been paid, in place of the ranch. She would not be able to run the ranch herself, and she would have to employ a manager, someone with experience. The stock we run there now is not enough to feed five people and employ a manager. We supplement our managers' wage from the hotel earnings.

The ranch belongs to Sandro. Even if Tomas had survived, he would not have been given the ranch. You heard his mother say that. It was always going to be Phillipe's, then Sandro's, and then our son's as it has been for generations of Rodrigos!'

'Bravo, Bethany!' they all said.
'Well spoken', said the judge.

As they were leaving, Bethany asked Grandmother whether she would like to come to the ranch next weekend. She was blessed with a delighted reply. 'Yes, Bethany, I have not been to the ranch since Phillipe was shot, and I have missed it many times. Listening to my nephew saying how he enjoyed his time there made me very nostalgic for those happy years we had. Thank you for your invitation, my dear. I shall look forward to it all week.'

'We shall pick you up on Friday at four o'clock, Grandmother. Take care till then. We all love you.'

On Tuesday morning, Judge Mendoza rang to say the clinic results had been completed and would be couriered to Señor Lazar's office that day.

'Could we all gather at the judge's office on Wednesday at 10 a.m. to hear the verdict and go on then to the next step?'

Bethany turned to Sandro and hugged him. 'What good connections your grandmother has! It will not be long now.'

The group gathered in the judge's boardroom. All looked apprehensive until the judge appeared, beaming, 'You were right!' he said. 'The results show without a doubt that Sandro is not related to the Horta family! I have asked Señora Horta to come here at eleven o'clock with her lawyer, to give her that information. Meanwhile, my secretary is organising coffee and cake for you. It should be champagne, but we thought it a little early in the day for that.' They all cheered.

When Terese Horta came into the room, looking self-important, with her lawyer in tow and saw everyone smiling and chatting, she hesitated just inside the door until Judge Mendoza motioned them in to a chair.

The judge then asked Sandro to tell the whole story again for the benefit of Terese and her lawyer.

When he was finished, Terese was white and shaking with fury, and she shouted, 'It is all lies! Maria told me it was Tomas, and the DNA she took proved it!'

The judge looked around at the group who were very quiet and then signalled Señor Lazar to show the letter from Doctor Donati and the brief from Grandmother Rodrigos and then the clinic results taken that week.

The judge turned to her and said, 'Señora Horta, this evidence is irrefutable. I am sorry there is no case for you. You have been severely misinformed by your mother-in-law. However, if you continue, I believe there is a kidnapping charge to be answered. There are no time limitations on kidnapping a child, also an extortion case of $300,000 US.

'Señora Bethany Rodrigos is willing to drop these charges against you if you cooperate and neither you or any of your children ever contact the Rodrigos family again. If you are interested, they believe there could be a person of interest who may be the children's grandfather. It has not been proved yet, so it would be up to you to follow it up. As you can have no contact with the family, perhaps your lawyer can follow it up with their lawyer. It is entirely up to you. If you still want your day in court, I must warn you that if you lose the case, you will have to pay all the court costs and charges.'

By the end of this Terese was weeping. Maria had misled her too. What damage can one mistake make? It just multiplies, and so many people get hurt.

After Terese and her lawyer had left, Sandro invited everyone to lunch at the restaurant that had become their favourite, the one they had gone to and enjoyed so much on Bethany's second evening in Buenos Aires.

Sandro announced during the lunch that his family would be going on a holiday to visit his sister in Paris and would then be visiting Bethany's family in Western Australia, just as soon as they could arrange it!

Señor Lazar looked at Bethany and smiled. She said, 'Thank you, Father Lazar, for believing in me.'

'What was that you called the señor, Bethany?' asked Sandro.
'I have decided to adopt Señor Lazar as my surrogate father. He has given us such wonderful advice over the years I have been in Buenos Aires, acting just like my father would. In consequence, he is also surrogate grandfather to Robert and Gina.'

Grandmother said, 'How nice you are, Bethany! That is a lovely thing to say.'

Sandro said, 'Yes, I agree. His advice has saved us many times. Also, he is somewhat like your father, Bethany, so it is OK with me.' He paused for effect and said slowly, 'It does mean we have reduced rates for family from now on, of course, señor.'

Everyone laughed at this. Sandro turned to the judge. 'Please visit us at the ranch when we return from our holiday and relive your youth. I will give you a call when we return and make a date.' And to Señor Lazar, he said, 'The same goes for you, señor. You are welcome to visit your grandchildren any time.'

The party broke up with handshakes and kisses and smiles, all promising to be in touch soon.

Two weeks later they were on their way, to Paris first, and went to the airport. For the first time the four of them travelled together.

Chapter 16

Bethany and Alessandro Rodrigos and their children Robert, aged five, and daughter Gina, aged almost three, landed at Charles de Gaulle Airport in Paris, tired from their flight but excited about their coming holiday in Paris. Sandro had wanted to visit his sister and her family for some time. It had not been possible until now because his father's care had taken first place for him for so long.

Ana had left her family home in Buenos Aires in Argentina many years before to follow a modelling career. She had married a French doctor, Pierre Dumont, and had two children and never returned to her homeland.

As they went to the immigration counter, an official approached the family and asked them to follow him to an office nearby, adjacent to the immigration counter. He called a man to take care of their luggage and showed them through the door.

Sandro and Bethany wondered what was going on. Were they to be searched for drugs? Or weapons? Knowing that would not be fruitful, they were curious to see why they had been pulled aside.

The official introduced himself as a policeman, asked by his superiors to advise the Rodrigos family of some details of the Dumont family.

By this time Sandro was uneasy about what the man was going to say. What had happened to his sister that a policeman was calling them aside? Was she OK? Was she in trouble? Maybe she had an accident? His mind was racing.

Some seats were found for them to fit into the small office. The policeman introduced himself as Inspector Martin Moreau, then explained that Ana Dumont was not able to meet them at the airport, and he had been given the job by his superiors of explaining some facts to them until Madam Dumont was able to contact them herself.

'Pierre Dumont is a doctor as you know. What you do not know is that he is deeply imbedded into the French Government terrorist detail. Because of his skills with languages, as he had travelled a lot with his father, who was also a doctor, into the Congo, to Morocco, and other countries. When as a child, he had gone to school in many different areas.

He had a knack for languages, picking up various dialects from the children at schools from various countries in Africa.

'He had been introduced into the terrorist team as a doctor to infiltrate the parts of Paris where these people lived. There had been many plots against the government, and Pierre had been very effective in the hunt for terrorists and plotters in general.

'Pierre Dumont spoke only French when dealing with the locals, and they were unaware that he understood everything around him that they said in their own languages. During the recent bombings in Paris, Doctor Dumont was called out to attend a slum area to help a wounded man who had escaped through the police net. Thanks to Doctor Dumont! He was picked up later, though no one suspected the doctor had been involved.

'During his ministrations to the wounded man behind a screen, he heard the other men talking in the room. This time they were talking about abducting Pierre and smuggling him to Syria, to help the fighters. They also said they would take the doctor's daughter. Here they laughed, saying what fun could be had with her. She was a beautiful nubile girl and just what the slavers were looking for. They could keep Pierre under control by threatening to sell her to the slave market. They liked girls that age.

'Pierre had been doing this work for us for many years, but now wanted to go on witness protection with his family. Your letter, sir, to your sister has put a cat among the pigeons, as they say. The whole family was being followed by the terrorists, and we, the police, are following the terrorists!

'It would make a good comedy if it wasn't so serious! If you showed up at the Dumont house, they would start following you. You could be in danger! We cannot pick up these terrorists yet, as they have done nothing so far, and they would be back on the streets within days. It would also give Doctor Dumont away, and his life would not be worth much after that.

'Now you understand our dilemma. We have booked you into a luxury hotel at the government's expense for a week. The Dumonts can meet you for dinner there each evening. Be discreet. Do not discuss anything I have told you while you are in the dining room. You do not know who is listening, no matter what language you speak. I am sure there is a lot you can talk about of Argentina and in your personal life to keep you going and to sound authentic. After dinner, go to your room and you can discuss it, though you should put the television on to cover your voices.'

The Rodrigos family were amazed at all that he revealed. Ana had never mentioned Pierre's work in her letters. She had only written once a year on Sandro's birthday; otherwise she never contacted them, so they knew virtually nothing of Pierre.

Monsieur Moreau continued, 'We have a hotel car waiting for you to take you to your residence for the next week, so if you go back out to immigration, you will find someone with a placard with your name on it, and you can return to just being tourists again. I hope you enjoy your holiday in our fair city. There is a lot to see and do here. It is not all gloom and doom. That is mainly hidden away.'

They thanked the policeman for the way he had handled the information and took their leave. The hotel driver was waiting as he said. They pointed their luggage out to him and were then driven through an amazing amount of traffic to the hotel. The hotel was quite central, which they thought was great. With two young children it would not be so hard to get around. They had brought a light stroller for Gina, but Robert would have to walk until he got too tired and then he would have to be carried.

They decided to put the children to bed and then have a rest themselves, so they would be alert for the dinner with the Dumonts. They found they could not settle. The news had been so unexpected that they were worried about the threat to Ana's family's safety and for their future. Perhaps it was lucky that they arrived when they had. At least they would know that they had gone into witness protection; otherwise it would be as if they just vanished.

The evening seemed to drag on forever for them, waiting for eight o'clock to come around. At last the Dumonts appeared, and they were seated at a table in an alcove, a little isolated from the other tables, not obviously so but cleverly so that they were away from other patrons.

Bethany and Sandro had recognised Ana immediately, even after she had been gone from Argentina for so long. Bethany recognised her from the magazine photo that Sandro had showed her. She was still beautiful. She was almost as tall as Sandro, and Bethany thought she looked very much like her mother Sofia; whereas Sandro looked like his father Phillipe.

Pierre was also tall, with a slight round to his back, a little older than his wife, Bethany guessed. He had a kindly appearance in his expression, and dark eyes that were very alert. His hair was dark, with sprinkles of grey at the temples. He was not a handsome man but somehow drew attention to himself by his self-effacing manner.

The children, Tamara and Julian, were perhaps eleven and nine, Sandro could not remember exactly. They were also tall for their ages. Tamara looked like her father and Julian looked very much like a Rodrigos, Sandro in particular.

They gave the usual French greeting, kisses on each cheek and shaking hands. Sandro longed to hug his sister but resisted in case they were being watched, as it could bring trouble later.

After ordering dinner, Pierre apologised to them that a family reunion, much looked forward to, would have to be conducted like this!

Sandro, prepped by the official at the airport, then went into the story of Sofia and Phillipe's deaths. Ana had only received a death notice in the mail at that time. He went through the whole story of how it had come about and its conclusions just a few weeks ago.

He described their life in Buenos Aires and told Ana that her grandmother was still alive and doing well and that she was living in a retirement village and was well and alert.

He also told her that they now rent out the town houses, how the hotel, owned jointly by Bethany and him, was doing well and now the ranch was really his, that he was thinking of putting chalets for holidaymakers to rent on the property.

At last he ran down. Their meal was finished by that time, and instead of ordering coffee, Pierre suggested they go up to their suiteto catch up and he would go to the bar and order drinks to be sent up. The younger children could go to bed, and the older ones could watch TV.

He went to the bar as he suggested, and the others went to the lift to go to their suite. Sandro had not noticed anyone suspicious hanging around but accepted he was a novice in the spy game.

As soon as they entered into the room and closed the door, Sandro hugged his sister. She laughed, a deep throaty sound, and hugged back, saying, 'Hola, little brother, not so little now! I am so happy to see you have found a wife, so beautiful, and your children are darlings and so well behaved. I have thought of you many times, caught up in Father's drama, hoping you could escape and make a life for yourself, and it seems you have, though a bit later than I had hoped for you. I have never wanted to return to Argentina. I think of myself as a Parisienne.

'Now and until this last week we have never wanted to change our lives. However, we are now caught up in a demented war that is here in Paris, growing daily. The average person does not realise. Now they want to abduct Pierre and take Tamara as well. We cannot stay and allow this to happen. Would you be willing to take Tamara and Julian with you when you leave Paris? I do not know when we will see them again. It is terribly unsafe for them at the moment, as Tamara has become a target, and Julian also if they cannot get to Tamara.

'I will stay with Pierre. I cannot imagine life without him. He is my life, my lover, and my friend, so I will have to give up my children for him. I will not allow him to be abducted by these crazy people. We never did think the children would be involved!

'You do not have to answer my plea to take the children yet. I know what a burden I am asking of you. It is a spur-of-the-moment thought at the moment when I saw how well you managed your own children. Pierre does not know about it yet, and I haven't thought it through properly. We are still waiting for the request for witness protection to come through from above. If they do not hurry up, it may be too late!

They promised an answer in a week, so you would know what has happened to us, as you are my only family. The reason you were contacted at the airport is, the letter you sent to us was opened by them – part of the 'Looking after' plan I suppose. We have bugs all over the house, and we are watched night and day. You get used to it, but it is annoying. Pierre is apparently one of their most successful spies, and they want to look after him. This abduction thing has only come up recently, and it has jolted them to think a doctor can be abducted and taken to a war zone. I think they never expected that to happen. And to think that they have included Tamara in their plan is obscene!'

Sandro was visibly upset by his sister's tirade. 'Ana, we will do what you want. If you want us to take the children with us, then we will do it. That is right, isn't it, Bethany?'

She nodded, and he went on, 'We will do our best for them as long as necessary, but why don't you consider all of you coming to Argentina?'

'Pierre is a patriot of France. I know he will not leave if he knows the children are safe, and I shall remain with him. I know he will want to go on with his work!' She added, 'We will have dinner each night this week. This will give the children time to get to know you and that we trust you. We have been told that we have one week to make a decision.

Go out and enjoy Paris by day, and we will meet here again every evening. I am sorry that I can't show our beautiful city to you. It is better I am not seen with you, but you will get an idea how lovely it is, and you can come back at a more auspicious time to take the remainder in.

'I wonder where Pierre has got to? He should be here by now. I will ring the bar and see if he is still there.'

She rang the reception desk, and they put her through to the bar.
After asking the barman if Pierre was there, he was speaking to her, asking if she had a nice time catching up with her old friends. Was she ready to go home yet? 'The children must be tired. I have been talking to Ahmed from Morocco staying at the hotel too. Are you ready to go home yet? Shall I come up, or shall I meet you at the lift?'

Sandro travelled down in the lift with his sister, and when they reached the ground, Pierre whispered, 'Be careful of this man Ahmed. You will recognise him by his bushy beard and eyebrows. He could be dangerous!'

Sandro stepped backwards into the lift and pressed the button to go up, saying to himself, 'What have we got caught up in? I wouldn't have expected this turn of events in a thousand years!'

****

The next morning, after breakfast at the buffet in the hotel, they caught a cab to the Eiffel Tower. 'Everyone has to see that once in their lives', said Bethany.

She had been gone there several years ago with her brother Mark. Their father had given them three months in Europe as a graduation present – Bethany from university and Mark from medical school.

Robert enjoyed going up and down in the lift but was not interested in the views, although Sandro was mesmerised by it. They spent most of the day there and caught a cab back to the hotel for the children to rest before dinner.

There was a note for them at reception when they went to pick up their key card. It was from Martin Moreau, the policeman from the airport, suggesting, 'Have dinner in your room tonight, ordering from room service.' He would smuggle Pierre and Ana and their children in the back way and up the stairs. He had noticed Ahmed in the bar last night, and he looked like a person of interest!

Sandro wondered where the inspector had been last night. He hadn't seen him!

The Dumont family arrived at 8 p.m., accompanied by Martin Moreau. When Sandro looked down the passage, he saw a man at each end of the passage and one at the lift. He raised his eyebrows at the inspector, who nodded and said, 'It is better to be safe than sorry.'

He came into the room with the Dumonts, saying, 'Just a few words before your dinner. Madam Dumont has suggested to us that you take their children with you to Argentina. She and her husband will stay in position here in Paris. I would like to confirm with you that it is your wish? You have not had very long to think about it.'

'Anything that will help my sister, Inspector. The children are welcome with us until it is safe to return them.'

Moreau looked at him with raised eyebrows. 'It may be a long time, sir. We are up against a hidden enemy imbedded amongst the general population. It is up to Pierre and Ana to say when they want out. Doctor Dumont is a patriot for France. That cannot be acknowledged because of the secret nature of his work. He is very important to us, though it is up to him to pull the pin if he wants out. One thing I must inform you of is the man Ahmed, who was in the bar last evening, checked into the hotel whilst the Dumonts were having dinner with you. So it seems he was following them. There was another man earlier following them, and he made a phone call, so we think that Ahmed has been set in place for the abduction. I do not think all of you are targets. There would be no point in it. They are here for the doctor and his daughter. We have the men in the passage now, and they will stay as long as the doctor is in the room. We will be back when the doctor rings, to escort him home. Goodnight for now.'

Sandro looked at his sister and her husband. 'So this is your decision then. You are all welcome to come to Buenos Aires. It is safe there. I know it is not Paris, but sometimes you have to make decisions for the family rather than the work. You could always come back to Paris when the danger has gone. They will find another doctor if you are not there.'

'Sandro, we have talked it over most of the night. We know it is dangerous. They only want Pierre because he is a doctor. They haven't discovered his other reasons for working in that area. The fighters in Syria and elsewhere are in need of medicos to patch them up and send them back to the fighting. If we can trick Ahmed into making a move towards Pierre, we may catch them out and thwart them. They do not know that we know about them.'

Sandro looked at her for a while and said, 'I can see that you have made up your minds about all this. We will play our part and take the children and care for them until you come and get them.'

By this time, the children were all asleep, and Bethany suggested having dinner from room service. After dinner, when Pierre and Ana were ready to leave, Bethany suggested leaving the children to sleep overnight. Perhaps the children could go with them tomorrow; they were going on a boat up the Seine. The children might enjoy a day out. They did not expect Sandro's family to be followed, so they could relax and enjoy themselves and get to know one another.

The children spoke French, some English, and some Spanish, but Bethany's French was very rudimentary, learnt at school and not spoken since, so she hoped they would understand each other. Ana and Pierre agreed and went home with their followers.

Next day, as they arranged, Sandro, Bethany, and the four children set off on their river cruise. The day was sunny and warm. It was not high season yet, so the boat was not crowded, and they had room to move about.

The children spent most of the time playing with each other, while Sandro was awestruck by bridges and buildings, especially the Notre Dame. They had a light lunch in a cafe at Mont Marte and then returned once more to the hotel in late afternoon for the smaller children to rest.

The children were exuberant coming back into the hotel foyer, and Bethany noticed that several people turned to look at them, including Ahmed, who was reading a newspaper in the central entryway. She also noticed that when he recognised them, he immediately stood up and walked to the lifts. She could not see which floor he had gone to, but she felt very alert for danger.

Meanwhile, Sandro had picked up the key cards for their suite, and the six of them made their way to the lifts.

On the way up, Bethany did not say anything, because she did not want to alarm the children that Ahmed may be waiting for them. When the lift door opened at their floor, she made certain that she was the last to leave the lift, and as she stepped out, she pressed the button to send the lift back downstairs to the ground floor.

Sandro had taken the stroller with Gina in it to the door of their suite and was inserting the key card into the slot. The two boys were following Sandro, but Tamara had hung back a bit to wait for Bethany.

Bethany saw Ahmed come out of a shadow of a doorway and grab Tamara. Half-expecting it, Bethany had her phone out and took a photo of Ahmed holding Tamara around her waist and holding a knife to her neck.

She spoke quietly to Tamara, so as not to alarm Ahmed and give him a reason to use the knife. She spoke in Spanish, hoping the Moroccan man did not understand. 'Keep very still, Tamara. Do not worry. I will deal with this man. I will not let him harm you. Can you pretend to faint? Just go loose at the waist so that he has to hold you up. That will give him just one arm to use. Good girl! Just move to the left a bit if you can. Well done!'

Whilst she was still talking, she had moved slowly towards them, and as Tamara folded, she reached out and grabbed the man's arm and jerked the knife away and the knife fell on the floor. Using her karate moves she had the man backed up to the wall, clutching his groin and knees and roaring.

Sandro had watched for a few seconds while this was happening and then he ran to help Bethany hold the man. Tamara crawled out between their legs, sobbing.

Bethany dialled Inspector Moreau's telephone number and explained what had happened. He must have got on to the hotel security because they came rushing up the stairs, showing their credentials. They held Ahmed until the inspector and his policemen appeared. The policemen took Ahmed away, and another policeman was delegated to search Ahmed's room at the hotel for drugs, syringes, or anything else they could find. They may have meant to hold Tamara drugged while they approached Pierre. Hiding in full sight did not work out for Ahmed!

Moreau and Sandro were very impressed with Bethany's performance.

Sandro was saying, 'Wow, Bethany, I did not know you could do that! I remember you telling me when we first met that you had a black belt in karate. It had not registered with me because I have never seen you doing it, and you are still able to do it after all this time!'

'I practise every day, Sandro, after you have gone to work. Gina and I do our exercises. You should see her. She is a mini expert at it. We shall show you sometime. Robert has not been as interested in the practice. He is far more interested in what Manuel is doing or playing with his toys.'

Inspector Moreau said, 'I commend you, madam. You nipped the operation in the bud, but this is the first action against the Dumonts. We did not expect it so soon. I do not think we can rest on our laurels just yet. I think Ahmed acted quickly without thinking it through. The opportunity came up and he took it. You cut off his escape by sending the lift down, which he wouldn't have expected. Also, he would have not expected a woman to attack him. A lose, lose situation for Ahmed.'

Bethany replied, 'I also have a photo of him on my phone, holding Tamara with a knife at her neck. You can charge him as a paedophile attempting to abduct a young girl. That will not appear as if Pierre is involved in any way. She was out with friends on a day trip, so Pierre can continue his work, and his patients from the community he works in will give him sympathy.'

'Madam, I am impressed with your abilities and mental acumen. Thank you for your quick thinking. Perhaps if I may borrow your phone for an hour I can go to headquarters and copy that photo. At this stage, I do not trust anyone else, so I will do the copy myself. Someone on my team must have notified the terrorist follower of the Dumonts where they were headed for Ahmed to get to the hotel so quickly the other evening. Not a good state of affairs!

'What are your plans for tomorrow?' The policeman asked.

Sandro answered, 'We are booked for a coach tour of Versailles. Do you think Tamara and Julian should come too? Ana has told me that she is having self-defence lessons. She might want to come to watch over Tamara and Julian. It seems to me the safest place. Surely, they cannot be aware of our plans that well. We only made the booking this morning.'

Moreau said, 'I am not sure of Madam Dumont's movements for tomorrow. Perhaps we can discuss it this evening when I deliver them for dinner. They would have to bring fresh clothes for the children. They stayed unexpectedly last night. I do like your idea, though. It would give us a day off from watching out backs.'

He went off with Bethany's phone, promising to deliver it back when he brought the Dumonts for dinner.

Tamara and Julian and Robert had been watching the television while this conversation had taken place. Gina had taken herself off to bed; she was still in need of a daily sleep.

Bethany went to Tamara and asked her how she was feeling.

Tamara answered, 'I was scared when the man grabbed me, and I was scared of the knife, but as soon as you started talking to me in Spanish, I calmed down. I did what you asked me to do, and I was not scared anymore. You seemed to be in charge, and you spoke so quietly, so I just pretended that we were in a movie. Was I all right? Also, I had to concentrate on what you were saying. Maman used to speak to us in Spanish when we were little, but when we started school, that became less and less, so I am a bit rusty. But you spoke slowly, and I was able to understand. It didn't seem as bad when I was pretending. I like acting. Do you think I would do well?'

'Tamara, you were wonderful! It was a bit like a movie scene, so we will think of it as that, shall we? The police have taken the man away, so we do not have to worry about him anymore. You go on with your television, and I will call down to room service for your meal. It is too late for you at eight-thirty when the grown-ups are eating, and I am sure you are very hungry. What would you like?'

The children all asked for hamburgers and French fries, so Bethany ordered four serves and went to wake up Gina.

They all showered and changed, except there were no clean clothes for the Dumont children. At least they would feel clean and fresh. They chatted while they waited for Ana and Pierre and Inspector Moreau, who all turned up at eight o'clock.

The children had tired while waiting, so they went off to bed, leaving Tamara to greet her parents.

Ana and Pierre were anxious to question their daughter on her attempted abduction this afternoon and whether she had any anxious after-effects from the ordeal.

They were satisfied with Tamara's calmness and her explanation that she had pretended she was playing in a scene from a movie and Aunt Bethany had saved her.

Ana turned to Bethany. 'I am so jealous that it was you who saved Tamara. You are so petite, one would not believe that you could overpower a big man holding a knife and save the child! You are absolutely incredible, Bethany. Thank you very much! I will have to continue my self-defence lessons. If you can do that, perhaps in time I may be able to do it.'

Pierre looked into Bethany's eyes and said, 'Thank you, Bethany.' It made her feel as if his whole soul was in those few words.

Inspector Moreau gave Bethany her phone, after showing the Dumonts the photo of Ahmed holding Tamara around the waist and with a knife held to her throat. He said, 'I have shown this photograph to my bosses at headquarters, and they concur with you, Bethany, that we charge Ahmed with child abduction and paedophilia. That should keep him locked away for a while.

'It does not stop there, though. There must be many ready to continue their course and try for Pierre's abduction. Someone up the top of their list has ordered this, and they will continue! We do know now that Tamara and Julian are safe in your care, and it will lift a lot of worry from Pierre and Ana.'

Ana asked, 'Have you done this sort of thing before, Bethany? Use karate, I mean?'

'When I was sixteen, my mother died. I sat around feeling sorry for myself for a couple of years and put on weight. When I started at university, I decided to take up running to lose weight. My father insisted that I learn karate as a self-defence, as I was running around parks alone most of the time. One day I was tackled by a man who came out of the bushes at me. His intention was rape. However, he found himself on the ground, squirming as Ahmed was this afternoon, and I blew my whistle. A group of us had got together and agreed to carry whistles and blow them if we were in trouble. If anyone heard the whistle, they would converge on the whistler. This time I was lucky. Three burly men turned up and held the antagonist until the police arrived and took him away. They did a DNA test on the man, and he was charged with raping a woman in that same spot six months previously. If we are to have your children for any length of time, I will teach them karate. They could be taught by Gina. She is an ace!'

Ana said, 'I am sure Tamara will be keen after today, now that she has seen you in action.'

Sandro said, 'I feel left out of the conversation. I did not even see Ahmed until he roared, and by then all the work had been done by Bethany! Perhaps I will learn karate as well.'

Bethany laughed. 'You are welcome to join our classes, Sandro. Perhaps Robert may start having an interest if you and Julian are learning. It is a wonderful way to keep fit and alert.'

Pierre, mostly silent until now, said, 'I think I will learn it as well, beside Ana. Who knows when it could come in handy?'

Sandro asked Inspector Moreau to join them for dinner so they could discuss their next moves.

Tamara went to bed after kissing her parents goodnight, in pyjamas this time.

Sandro rang room service and ordered meals for five. While they were waiting for the meal to arrive, Sandro asked Ana if she would join them on the coach trip to Versailles the next day.

Ana looked at Pierre. 'Why not both go? Surely you can take a day off from work if your daughter had an abduction trauma at knife point?'

The men all laughed, and Pierre said, 'It seems like a good idea to me. What about it, Inspector? Would you join us, so that you and Bethany can keep us safe?'

Everyone laughed this time, just as their room service trolley was wheeled into the room. So it was arranged that they would all go to Versailles the next morning. Inspector Moreau accompanied Pierre and Ana home, leaving the children to sleep the night in the hotel again.

****

Nothing was said as they went through the magnificent rooms of the palace. They were all caught up in the beauty of it. Even the children were quiet as they traversed the rooms. The group had spread out a little. By the time they had reached the gardens, Bethany found herself walking with the inspector and asked of him,

'Did you find anything incriminating in Ahmed's bedroom at the hotel?'
'There was a syringe and a drug there, and it has been sent off for analysing. We at headquarters think Ahmed was going to abduct Tamara and give her the drug by injection to keep her quiet, until they got both Pierre and Tamara away, possibly by ship, we are not sure of that yet. They could not wait too long, as it is very expensive to hold a ship in port, so we think the timing must be soon for them to contact Pierre.

'Because Ahmed tried the snatch yesterday, we think it is scheduled to contact Pierre as soon as possible. We have Ahmed's phone, and we are tracing his calls and callers. His passport shows that he came to France two weeks ago. It is not his first visit. He has been here several times, although he is not registered as a citizen. It could be that he is a courier for ISAS. He is not saying anything at the moment, so it could be all conjecture. We are hoping something will come up on his phone records to give us a lead.'

'That is a chilling thought', said Bethany. 'I am glad I was able to be of help!'
'Your help, Madam Rodrigos, has been so important. We have Ahmed under lock and key with a charge he cannot beat. We have a photo of him holding Tamara and the hotel security squad as witnesses. With luck they may give up

the idea of taking Pierre to their war field hospital.'

Bethany turned to him and asked seriously, 'Can you keep my name out of the reports? Just say I was a tourist. We have these nasty people in Australia as well. Not so many of them, but enough that if names were mentioned, they could look us up, and it could be a problem for my family at home.'

'We have already thought of that and described you as a passer-by, a tourist that disappeared before you could be identified. Also, the hotel security took the photo when they were called to the scene, seconds before the rescue by the tourist.'

'Thank you for that, monsieur.'
'We have to wait and see what happens next. If you take the Dumont children when you leave Paris, it may be the end of it.'

'We are going to Australia first for two weeks, before returning to Buenos Aires. By then it may be all over. My family lives in Western Australia, and I haven't seen them for almost three years, so it will be a nice break. I cannot say that it has been a restful holiday so far.

'The extra children will not be a problem. My family will welcome them. They are nice children and will not be too much trouble. Tamara already trusts us, although Julian is too quiet. Perhaps he does not understand the difference in the languages as well as Tamara, but he will learn quickly, and it does not worry me. I am sure I can manage.

'We will be back in Buenos Aires in three weeks' time. Can you keep us updated from time to time? We will be in contact with Ana by phone. With the time difference, there will be a little trouble with that. Also, Ana is not much a correspondent. She only sent a letter to Sandro once a year. Thank you, Inspector, for warning us at the airport. It alerted me straightaway when I saw Ahmed get up and go to the lift before us. I would not have made anything of it if you hadn't warned us beforehand.'

Just then Sandro caught up with them and said, 'What are you two plotting? I have been talking to Ana and Pierre. They seem to be resigned that the children will be leaving with us. Such a sad state of affairs, hopefully not for long. Ana seems to think she will be going to work with Pierre as his nurse. Would she be safe, Inspector?'

'No one can say for sure. Pierre's work is very important, mainly because he understands the various languages. Ana does not have the languages, but she does have women's intuition that picks up oddities in daily life. That in itself could be an advantage when Pierre is busy.

'Pierre has never placed himself in danger. To these people he is purely a doctor. Ana will not have to be an actress, just a health worker assigned to Pierre to assist him. Unless they decide to abduct Ana as well, I do not see any danger for her. We do think she should wait for at least a month to allow the story of Tamara's abduction to die down. We will keep an eye on Pierre for that time. Possibly they will think it all too hard and give up.

'Not everybody in that area are suspects. Most of them are immigrants wanting to make a better life and bring their children up safely away from squalor and ignorance. The story of Tamara's fright may help Pierre to become more high profile amongst them and then he would become harder to snatch as a consequence. The children will be able to come home to their parents if there are no more murmurings going on. At this stage, we have no idea when that will be.'

Ana and Pierre and the children had caught up with them, and they started talking about when the Rodrigos group would leave France.

Moreau was of the opinion that the snatch group would try again and soon. If they had a ship waiting, it could not stay long because of the port charges; however, headquarters had not yet come up with a vessel and had no idea how they had planned to get clean out of France.

It would be better if they left the next day or two at the most. Tamara should not be put through it again. They may even try for Julian; he is lighter and easier to carry.

'Our original tickets were for another week. Are you sure, Inspector? We will ring them tonight to make new reservations for Tamara and Julian.'

'Don't worry, Madam Rodrigos. If you give me your tickets, we will approach the airline on your behalf and get the additional tickets and change the dates to what is available.'

Bethany took the airline tickets from her handbag and handed them to him and turned to Ana and said, 'Do you have the children's passports?'

Ana looked into her handbag and brought out the two passports and also a letter stating they gave permission for the children to leave France with the Rodrigos family. The letter was notarised, so she handed it all to the inspector.

'Good,' he said, 'I will get onto this as soon as we get back to Paris.'

The coach delivered them back to the hotel at five-thirty. They decided to go to a small cafe a short distance away, and the inspector rang for some policemen to stand by. It seemed that restaurants and cafe are targets nowadays.

The children were all tired. They had walked a lot around the palace and grounds, so they did not dally at the cafe, and they decided to have a quick meal and go their separate ways – Tamara and Julian to go with their parents this time. It would be the last they would see them for some while.

Sandro and Bethany strolled back to the hotel, with Robert standing on the step of the stroller because he said he was too tired to walk. Bethany found herself looking around at the people, not the place. She did not want to think of further trouble, but it would not leave her mind. Thankfully, nothing happened, and she realised that the whole Dumont thing had spoilt any sense of a holiday spirit. She loved Paris, although this time she would be glad to leave.

The inspector rang later to say that he was unable to change the booking for the following day. However, there was a flight the day after, and six business class tickets had been organised. The flight left at 9 a.m., direct Paris to Dubai, with a change of aircraft at Dubai and then direct to Perth.

They were to follow the normal route to the airport. The inspector would arrange for Tamara and Julian to board the aircraft beforehand, and he would wait with them until the Rodrigos family had boarded and were seated and the aircraft ready for departure.

So, they had one more day in Paris and decided to go on a coach tour around Paris and leave the coach at Sacré-Cœur and catch a cab back to the hotel, and have dinner quite early in the dining room so the children could join them.

Inspector Moreau said he would have a man in the bar just in case, and another on their floor until 9 p.m. The policemen would be back at again at 8 a.m. to help them with the departure to the airport.

They made the coach tour booking with the concierge at the hotel and went to their suite to shower and rest. It was tiring being a tourist. Robert and Gina seemed to manage quite well, though Gina often dozed off in the stroller.

They were picked up by the coach at 9 a.m. and saw the streets of Paris from the coach windows, realising the children would only see a sea of legs if they were walking around. There were so many people out there, it would be impossible for the children. At the magnificent Sacré-Cœur, they looked at paintings and statuettes and the painters and the general colourful scene. They had lunch in a busy small cafe, and coming out of the cafe, Robert said he was tired. Robert sat down on the wide steps and said he wanted to go home now! They realised that they were tired too, so they finished climbing down the steps and caught a cab back to the hotel.

Sandro commented, 'Maybe we have not seen everything, although we have tried to fit the important things in. But we shall come back when the children were older and be able to appreciate it.'

Ana, Pierre, and the children came to the hotel at 7 p.m. for dinner and left at 8.30 p.m. They would not see Ana and Pierre again until they came to pick their children up from their exile.

****

Sandro and Bethany spent the evening packing and discussing where they would stay when they arrived in Perth. Two extra people were a bit much to expect for their family to provide for, so they decided to find an apartment somewhere close to the city. Bethany went on to her computer and came up with just the thing, a three-bedroom apartment close to the city, with a kitchen if she wanted to make meals when the children were tired and to have breakfast at their own leisure!

The fares from Perth to Buenos Aires had still to be changed and added to; however, Bethany wanted to get a new phone. She still felt wary about trying to ring on her phone, which had been out of her possession for two hours. She did not want to leave a trail if anyone was trying to intercept. And as the inspector would have said, 'Better sure than sorry', she would wait until she was in Australia.

The next morning, when they arrived at the airport, they noticed extra policemen posted around. The boarding was normal with no one taking particular notice of them that they could see. Tamara and Julian were waiting in their seats,

152

and Inspector Moreau stood up and greeted them. It appeared natural and not out of the ordinary.

He shook hands and said, 'Thank you, Señor and Señora Rodrigos. We appreciate the part you have played in this emergency. Good luck and goodbye.' Then he was gone.

The flight to Dubai and then to Perth passed well. The children were happy playing games and watching movies on the flight computers. Sandro and Bethany were glad to have a rest. It had been a tumultuous week, with quite a lot of mental strain! Tiring as a tourist, all the people was a strain on its own. The added danger had made them feel strung up, and they only noticed it now that they were out of Paris and on their way to Australia. They all had a sleep on their last leg from Dubai to Perth so that they would not land in Perth worn out totally.

The apartment that Bethany had chosen was close to the city and it was a family hotel and it suited them well. She had not called her father yet. He was expecting them next week; the early departure from Paris had messed things up. They had been going to stay with her father and Jenny his wife, but they would contact them and tell the story of why they came earlier with two extra children.

But first she had to get a new phone, so her first thing in the city was to buy a new iPhone. She felt better after that. She felt as if she was starting a new chapter and no one could track her now. The strange feeling, she had while they were in Paris left her, and she felt liberated from the pressure of it.

She rang her father on the new phone and arranged to meet for dinner at a small restaurant close to his home. They picked up Bethany's car from the lock-up garage that it had been stored in whilst she was in Argentina. It was not an extra big vehicle, but they all managed to fit in with the two car seats necessary by law for Robert and Gina. It was a bit squashy, but they managed.

Tamara was a real boon when moving around, holding Gina's hand and chatting to her in Spanish. Julian was very quiet, not saying much at all. When Bethany got him by himself and asked him if he was unhappy, he burst into tears. 'I am afraid for my papa. The bad men are trying to kidnap him, like they did to Tamara!'

She knew this was his problem. She had been aware whilst they were together in Paris that no one seemed to notice that the children were listening to them.

She had tried to keep them away from the adults' conversation as much as she could, but Ana did not try to do so. She felt that only telling him the truth now could undo some of the damage.

'Yes, they are trying to kidnap him, but there are policemen watching over him all the time and the bad men might not be able to get to him. The bad men do not know that the policemen are watching your papa, so they might get caught first like Ahmed did when he tried to get Tamara. He is a big strong man, so he would be able to fight the bad men. It may all be over soon, and you will be able to go home again to your maman and papa. We have to wait and see, so while you are here with us we will take you to see some kangaroos, and maybe we will see some koalas too. We will go to the zoo, where all the children like to go, and tomorrow we might go to the museum and see some skeletons of dinosaurs. So try not to worry. We will have a good holiday and enjoy ourselves, and in a little while we will go on another aeroplane to fly to Argentine. That is the country where your Maman grew up, so that will be interesting for you to see.'

Julian's tears had dried up by now, and he was grinning. 'Papa said he was going to learn karate like you, so they will not get him!'

'That is right, Julian, so let's go to the zoo now. We will go on the ferry boat across the river to South Perth. The zoo is only a short walk from where we land.' She knew by then that she would not have any more trouble with him.

Several days of doing only children's things began to pall for Sandro, so they began to think of going home earlier to get back to normal.

Bethany's brother Mark asked, 'Would you be godparents to our twin sons at their baptism? They are eighteen months old now, and we have been waiting for you to visit and here you are!'

'Great!' said Bethany. 'When is it to be?'
'The priest at our church said anytime, if it was done during a normal service. However, if it is a private baptism, they would have to fit into the dates the priest has available. When do you plan on returning to Argentina?'

'As soon as the baptism is over', said Bethany.
'I will ring and organise a date. Laura and I prefer the family affair, as the boys are a bit of a handful. They egg each other on and unlike the calm personality of Robert. With these two you do not know what to expect.'

They had been having dinner at their father's house and were now sitting outside under the patio watching the boys kicking a football around. Mathew, Julian, and Robert were all hitting it off well. They were kicking an Australian rules football, which was an oval shape and much harder to manage than the round soccer football used in other parts of the world. Julian had told them that he played soccer at his school in Paris, and he was doing well with the ball for his first try. Everyone was cheering him on, and he was doing well until he kicked the football into the swimming pool. The boys all had fun getting it out of the pool.

It was a lovely day, and everyone was happy. What a contrast to the drama of the Paris adventure! It was lovely watching the children play. Mark and Laura's twins were playing by themselves, two little blond-haired children, a big contrast to Robert, Julian, and Tamara who all had dark hair and brown eyes. Uncle Mathew, as Robert called him, was also a blonde and was enjoying the company of the other children. He was now a school boy and had lost his first teeth and was growing the second ones.

Bethany was happy sitting with her father. It was wonderful being with her family. Her grandparents were not there; they would go and see them tomorrow. They were getting frail, both in their mid-eighties.

Everybody was interested in how they managed to double their family on a trip to Paris.

Sandro related the drama, and when he got to the part where Bethany saved Tamara by using her karate skills, he said, 'Thanks to you, Father Randford. Your diligence in making sure Bethany could look after herself saved Tamara from goodness knows what obscene future. We will look after them until it is safe to return.'

It seemed unbelievable to them. They had all been to Paris and loved it. It was a shame that the Parisians had to put up with the terrorist thing.

Tamara had stayed close to Bethany whenever they went out in public, and it occurred to Bethany that it was the Australian English language that she was hearing that made her a little nervous. Although she had learnt English at school, it was hard to understand the Australian accent. When she asked Tamara about this, she said she felt like an alien from another planet. She only understood a little of what people were saying.

Bethany laughed. 'Do you understand me when I speak English, Tamara?'

'Not always, but I seem to get the idea of what you are saying mostly. It is mostly guesswork, but you do not talk as fast as everyone else.'

'I will remember that and try and talk slower and softer. I have been aware since I have been here that everyone seems loud!'

The day came for the baptism of the twins, Damian and Ian. They were identical twins and looked cute in their little suits. They had all gathered at the church, all dressed up in their Sunday best. Bethany noticed a table at the back of the church with coloured pencils and paper and some toys. She pointed it out to Robert and Gina, and they made straight for it.

The service was short, as there was not the full mass, and the twins did behave. They seemed very interested in what was going on and did not squirm and cry as Mark had predicted. It was all quite charming, Bethany thought.

They thanked the priest, who declined the offered lunch, saying his duties for the day were not finished and blessed them.

The rest of the congregation made their way to Mark and Laura's house for a festive lunch and afternoon.

Sandro was starting to wonder how Daniel and Felix were managing at the hotel. Three weeks had passed and Bethany had noticed that he was ready to go back to work. It was the longest period of time that he ever been away from it.

When they arrived back at the apartment, she rang the airline to change their tickets and add two more, for the next day.

They had still not heard anything from Ana or Pierre, although it was two weeks since they had taken their children away from Paris. Bethany felt confused by this; it must be the Rodrigos way – out of sight, out of mind! Just like when she and Robert had come to Australia after Robert's kidnapping! She felt that she would be enquiring about her children if they were parted for even one day!

****

So, they were moving on again. This time when they would be arriving at the airport in Buenos Aires, there would be six of them.

Chapter 17

When the Rodrigos group arrived at Buenos Aires airport, they hired an SUV from the car hire agency to accommodate the family and their luggage, a substantial amount for six people.

On the way home they stopped at a supermarket to pick up fresh fruits and vegetables, milk, bread, and anything else Bethany could think of that she did not already have in her pantry. They had left home in a flurry and had not stopped to think what they needed when they got home.

When they got to their house, they all piled out of the car and went into the house, and Sandro called Manuel to help unload the luggage. They deposited the luggage at the foot of the stairs heading to the bedrooms. Sandro announced that he was going to the hotel to check on things and that he would be back in an hour.

Bethany decided a shower and fresh clothes was needed to freshen up, after the long flight. They raided the suitcases for clothes for Tamara and Julian. The rest of them had clean clothes in their rooms.

When they were fresh and clean, Bethany went into the kitchen and made scrambled eggs on toast and poured a glass of milk for the four children.

As they were finishing, there was a knock at the kitchen door as Sandro came into the room and announced, 'We have a visitor, everybody!'

They all looked at the doorway as Sandro's sister Ana entered. Tamara and Julian both yelped 'Maman' and then 'Papa?'

Ana entered and folded her children into her arms. She said, looking at Bethany, 'The terrorists have kidnapped Pierre, the day you left Paris. He went to work at the clinic to be there by 9 a.m. and disappeared!'

'Come, Ana,' Bethany said, 'sit down and tell us all about it.'
'Pierre went to work in his car, and about the time he would have arrived at the clinic, a bomb went off on a vacant block a few minutes down the road from the clinic, vacant because a building was bombed a year ago at that site. All the policemen ran down to the area and were gone only ten minutes. When the squad came back to the clinic, Pierre's car was there, unlocked, and Pierre was missing! The police are sure that the bomb going off was a diversion. It was timed very carefully to the minute, so they must have had someone following Pierre.

Inspector Moreau is very disappointed in his squad, but as he said, policemen are only human, and it is their job to investigate bombings and help if necessary. This time it was a hoax, to pull them away from the clinic.

'I did not let you know. You had your long-awaited Paris trip messed up for you. You were unable to do anything being so far away, so I waited to let you know. Inspector Moreau thought it better if I disappear too, in case they came back for me to persuade Pierre.

'I know how much of a doctor Pierre is. He would not refuse to help wounded, no matter what side they were on. He is a dedicated doctor, and he would follow the rules of the Hippocratic Oath at all times.

'I could see Inspector Moreau's concern. I would have to be overseen by the police day and night. A lot of manpower had gone into protecting Pierre, yet the terrorists won and still evade them. Because the police play by the rules, and for the terrorists there are no rules.

'Anyway, it seemed to me that Paris was just a place. Without Pierre and the children there was nothing to keep me there. Moreau wanted me to disappear, so I did! I have been a week here now, staying at your hotel, which is very nice. I have wandered about a bit. I looked at the town houses from the outside. I wanted to visit Grandmother, but I had no idea where to find her. I have neglected her so long now. I do not know what sort of reception I would get from her.

'Can I rent one of the town houses from you, Sandro? If I am staying with the children, I will have to arrange schools and longer visas. I now travel on a French passport, the same as the children, as you know. I do not know how long we will be here, until Pierre is released. That could be months or years, nobody knows. I had thought of going to Syria to find him. Moreau talked me out of it. He said he may not be in Syria. There is fighting in many places over the world, and he could be anywhere!'

Sandro said, 'You can have one of the town houses, Ana. You do not have to pay rent! However, I will have to check the bookings to see if we can cancel something first. They have been very popular and have hardly ever been vacant. Do you want to stay here with us or at the hotel until we are able to accommodate you in a town house when one becomes vacant? Julian can share Robert's room, Tamara can share with Gina, and we have one more guest room for you if you want to stay a while.'

'Thank you, Sandro and Bethany. I know I am a nuisance. I just do not want to be alone yet. The shock of not having Pierre with me is hard to bear. I feel like breaking down about every two hours. Having you all around me will help me cope with the fact that he has gone and may never come back. I have to be like the millions of other women who saw their husbands off to war, not knowing whether they would ever see them again.'

Sandro said, 'Ana, we know this is hard for you. We know you love Pierre. You now have to concentrate on your children! Making a good life for them. Remember, they have lost their father, whom they love as much as you do. I want you to act cheerful, even if you feel like crying, for their sakes! Remember when our father was shot? Everybody looked after him. Nobody considered how it affected us, the children reaching the years when they needed guidance!

I became his slave and you left home, never to return. You must consider your children and put your grief aside. Learn from your experience. You are not the only one to miss Pierre in their lives.'

Tamara came and kissed her uncle Sandro and whispered to him, 'Maman only cares for Papa. She was always jealous of the time he spent with Julian and me!' Out loud she said, 'We have enjoyed our holiday in Western Australia, Maman. Now we have to learn about Argentina, where you grew up. That is very exciting.'

Julian piped up, 'Aunt Bethany says that Papa can look after himself. He is a very strong man!'

Ana looked at Bethany. 'The subject has already come up?'
Bethany nodded. 'It may crop up again from time to time. We must stay positive.'

'How fortuitous that you came to Paris when you did! You have been a tower of strength to us, both of you. We have lost Pierre to the terrorists, but thanks to you, Bethany. We still have Tamara, for which I shall be forever in your debt. OK, what do you want me to do first?'

Bethany smiled. 'That is the spirit. We have to reorganise the beds for three extras. Come, I will show you around.'

The children all followed, and they went upstairs to the bedrooms.

Bethany turned to Tamara. 'I am sorry that you will have to share with Gina. She is an early bird, so if she wakes you in the morning too early, send her out to me and go back to sleep.'

' It will not be a problem for me, Aunt Bethany. I like to get up early myself. Can we start karate lessons tomorrow morning?'

' Yes, Tamara, we would start before breakfast around 7.30 a.m. We will only do half an hour – the first fifteen minutes limbering up, the second doing moves. We do not want to overwork you to get too tired. After a couple of weeks, we can extend it to do a little longer as you get fitter.

'The first thing to remember about karate is that it is an art that involves the mind, the body, and the spirit. The body must remember how to move, and the mind, in turn, must remember to be still. It is a courteous art, and while we practise it, we must be sure not to harm each other.'

'Can I join in too?' asked Ana.

'Of course, you can if you wish. You boys too. That includes you too, Sandro. You said you want to learn.'

'I have to go to the hotel early tomorrow morning to see what is needed and to catch up.'

'I know, Sandro, but you can spare half an hour. Or shall I call you a wimp?'

Sandro laughed. 'OK, include me in. At least, except for Gina, I will not be the only first-timer.'

Everyone was tired by now. Jet lag was catching them up, except for Ana, so Bethany shooed the children to their beds, promising prayers tomorrow night before bed.

The adults went back to the kitchen to have their meals and then went to bed also.

The next morning, as promised, Bethany lined them all up on the back veranda of the house to commence the first karate lesson. Gina stood in front with Bethany to show what could be done. Although she was so tiny, she was really good at it, and all the others came to kiss them both when they had finished the half hour.

Bethany congratulated all of them. 'We will be a surprise if anyone attacks us', she said. 'We need a lot more practices, so we will be back here tomorrow at 7.30 a.m. You can practise whenever the mood gets you. It is an art that needs to be done often to help the muscles and the memory.'

They all went off to breakfast with satisfied looks on their faces. It was fun done in a group.

Sandro was happy that he had joined in. It had been fun, and now he was off to the hotel. Three weeks was the longest that he had been away from it, and he was anxious to see Daniel and Felix to see if there were any problems that had come up while he was away.

Bethany and Ana chatted about schools to enrol the children Robert would be starting in the next term as well, so they had a mutual interest.

First, they rang Grandmother and asked her to lunch the next day to meet Ana and her children.

Bethany rang Señor Lazar to say hello and to ask him about Ana's situation regarding getting her Argentina passport back and getting the same for Tamara and Julian. She asked him to lunch the next day as well.

The hired SUV came in handy. Sandro had taken his car to the hotel. He normally would have walked, but he had been in a hurry today. They all piled into the vehicle to go hunting for a school in the area and getting more provisions from the supermarket.

The school problem was fixed when they saw a new building with a substantial fence around it. They took a note of the name of the school for Bethany to look up more information on the Internet about it. They checked on the computer, and Ana was then all for going to see the headmaster to enrol the children. It was a big decision made, but Bethany said to wait for the children to get over the jet lag they must be feeling; they had just had a long flight and were sure to be tired for a day or two.

They also needed time to meet their great-grandmother Rodrigos the next day. Tamara and Julian would be having a little difficulty with the language and need clear heads for their first school days. It was as well that they now had Ana to tutor them in the evenings to catch up with a new curriculum.

Lunch the next day with Grandmother and Señor Lazar brought another surprise for them. It seems that Señor Lazar, whose name on his letterheads said Francis Lazar, was also Frank and had been the nurse for Phillipe Rodrigos.

He had been studying law at the time, and it was a good part-time job with housing supplied. He had taken the job because he was only needed for two hours in the morning and two hours in the evening, which gave him time to attend lectures and to study, and there was free housing supplied in the unit that was used by Sandro later. It was all ideal until he and Ana had started an affair and were discovered and he was dismissed.

Ana was taken aback – her one-time lover here to have lunch! She turned to Sandro and asked if he recognised Frank.

'No, I was at school or at the hotel, so I rarely saw Frank. So no, I did not recognise him.'

She turned back to Señor Lazar, as all the others called him. She went to him, and he held out his hand, looked at Ana and her children, and said, 'Hello, Ana, you have beautiful children. I am sorry that they are not mine too. I have never married.'

'Ana, for once in her life,' thought Bethany, 'was completely lost for words.'
Grandmother was pleased to see Ana and meet her children. She was aware of the friction in the air. She had lived in the town house during the period when Frank was there but had not recognised Frank. The Frank she remembered was a young muscly person who wore T-shirts and tracksuits. This Señor Lazar wore smart suits and had a distinguished air about him.

Señor Lazar went on to Ana. 'I am proceeding with immigration regarding your former passport, and there appears not to be any problem. The children's passports will follow after yours is established.'

Sandro said to him, 'You already knew about my father's problems. Why did you not say anything?'

Frank looked at him surprised 'I did not think it relevant. I was not involved with your problems at the time. I was a law student doing a part-time job, to pay for my studies. You may have taken offence for my association with Ana if I brought it up, and all for nothing to do with our dealings together.'

Bethany said, 'Yes, Sandro. I was the one to introduce Señor Lazar to our business dealings, if you remember. He was also the one I turned to for help. He knew me as Bethany Randford, and the Rodrigos bit came a little later, and by then I was sold on him, no matter what his former life.'

Señor Lazar and Sandro both laughed. 'Well spoken as usual, Bethany', said Sandro. 'Whatever I would do without you to bring me down to earth I do not know!'

'You are a seriously lucky man, Sandro, to have such a clever wife!' laughed Señor Lazar.

Ana had been quiet, listening to this exchange and wondering about their ease with one another. Grandmother too seemed at ease with Frank. It was enlightening to Ana.

Bethany never seemed to raise her voice and held the people together without any effort. Even the children were well behaved. At home, by now Julian would be jumping up and down, wanting attention, but Bethany just smiled and went on with doing things, and everybody was happy in her company. She could not remember the last time she felt so relaxed like this. Bethany was so right for Sandro; they made a handsome couple, and he seemed to adore her.

Even Tamara and Julian looked up to her. What a remarkable woman! She could not have found anyone better to look after her children, and now she was being looked after as well. All this from Sandro's wife! He was truly blessed!

Her thoughts ran on, and suddenly she realised that Frank was standing next to her, and she jumped.

Frank laughed. 'Ana, you are still beautiful! I am sorry about your husband. Sandro just told me the story. Would you come out to dinner with me? We could catch up from our early days. I would like to see you again. Would tomorrow be too soon?'

She looked at him. 'There has been a lot of water under the bridge since we saw each other last. Yes, tomorrow would be nice.'

'Then I will take you to the Rodrigos' favourite restaurant. Shall I pick you up at eight?'

The next evening, he called for Ana at eight as expected, and they went to the restaurant. Over dinner they discussed their lives. Frank explained that after Ana's father turned him out, he had gone to a friend's place first, then to a YMCA house with other students. He had little money, as his family could not support him, and most of the money he had earned had gone to pay for tuition and books. He had gone back to the Rodrigos' houses at least twice a week and waited outside, hoping to catch her come out.

'I never did,' she explained, 'because I had moved out to an apartment with three other girls. I had seen an advertisement in the "Homes to let" section of the newspaper, asking for a female roommate, so I had left the town house two days after you and never went back! I did not know how to contact you', she said, smiling. 'We did not discuss much. We were too busy getting to know each other in a different way.'

He answered, still smiling, 'I remember it well. No one I met later came anywhere near you, so I have never married. As I told Bethany, I was married to the law.'

They had discovered the old attraction was still there, as friends now.

Chapter

18

Six months later, Inspector Moreau contacted Ana by email. 'The hospital where Pierre was working had been bombed by Allied Forces and flattened. Anyone inside would have been killed. Pierre was declared missing, presumed dead. No one had heard from Pierre, so if he had escaped, he either did not have the means for communication or was wounded and perhaps recaptured. We will advise if any news comes to hand.'

Pierre had been working for six months now in the hospital for sixteen hours a day and then he was escorted by his captors to a bedroom and was locked up for eight hours to rest. He was fed well; he needed to keep his strength up for his work.

He had learnt the captors' language, easy for him. He did this second nature to him, hiding the knowledge that he could understand them, and they thought he had nothing but the necessary words to get by. He had a nurse assigned to him, a middle-aged woman named Latifa. She worked the same shifts with him and also helped when he was operating.

Pierre had not been fully trained as a surgeon, but fifty per cent of his duties now was to operate on someone, and he was getting quite good at it.

Latifa was a widow, perhaps in her middle thirties. Her husband had been killed in the early stages of the war.

Pierre found it easy to work with her. Her movements were quick and decisive, and she did not seem to tire easily. They were friendly. She was perhaps his only friend here because people seemed to come and go, and he never knew who would be facing him over the operating table. Sometimes it was just him and Latifa. Staff never seemed to last long, although the patients kept coming.

Latifa knew that Pierre could understand the languages spoken. She had dropped a surgical dish with instruments in, and she had been very distressed at the error. Pierre had bent down to help her pick up the instruments and whispered to her, 'Don't worry, Latifa. Everyone makes a mistake sometime, and it will not take long to sterilise the instruments again.'

She had been amazed to hear him, thinking he did not understand the language. He put his finger to his lips and smiled at her. She never told anyone.

Latifa came to his room one night. She had acquired a key from somewhere and unlocked the door. 'Please, Doctor, will you come to my house with me? My niece lives with me, and she has gone into labour. I cannot save the baby. It is in a breech position, and I cannot hear a heartbeat. Will you come? The staff here will not admit her, as she does not have a husband. So they will not allow her in. She was raped by her father's brother, and he made her pregnant. Her father turned her out, and the uncle remains! Her mother, my sister, asked if I would look after her, as otherwise she would be homeless and prey to any man!'

Pierre did not hesitate. He put his pillow and some clothes under a blanket to make it look like he was asleep and then picked up his medical bag and his coat with all his documents in the inside pocket and crept out with her. They went down long passages to a side door that opened to a car park, then hurried to Latifa's house, which was not too far away.

The girl Rahima was very distressed to see a man in her room. Latifa explained who he was. She was only fifteen and quite small. The baby just did not have room to move around. Pierre listened for a heartbeat but could not hear one. He asked Latifa when was the last time she heard a heartbeat.   She apologised and said that she had been so tired this week that she had not listened, thinking everything was fine.

Pierre examined her and agreed there was no heartbeat from the baby. Rahima was quite distressed. He decided, with Latifa, that the best thing to do was a Caesarean operation. He was not a surgeon, but his skills had been honed in the last six months, but he would have to be quick because he did not have the right anaesthetic for a prolonged operation.

After the operation, as they were cleaning up, they heard and felt an enormous explosion somewhere in the area in the direction of the hospital.

They went outside to investigate. They could see the whole area was flattened. Latifa grabbed his arm and said, 'Come back to my house quickly. They will not find you missing now. It is a good time to escape and go home to your own country.'

They went back to her house. Rahima was sleeping quietly, and they sat down to talk about it over a cup of mint tea.

They agreed that Rahima was in need of rest for at least three days. Latifa wanted to take Rahima away.

There were not too many honour killings nowadays, but Rahima's father was of the old ways. He and his brother may take into their minds that she had shamed them and come and hunt for Rahima. It had been done in other families, so she was not safe here; they had to go away.

'Will you let us come with you, Doctor? It will be a good disguise for you. We could pass as a family group. I have some of my husband's clothes here, so you can look the part. He was a tall man like you. You could say that your papers have been lost when your house was bombed, and in the fire, caused by it. You had no chance to rescue your identity papers.'

Pierre laughed. 'Are you sure, Latifa, that you did not order this bombing tonight? That is a quick observance of how we can escape!'

Latifa laughed too. 'No, sir, I did not arrange the bombing, but I have been looking for a chance to escape since Rahima came to me. I had to wait to save some money first and for the right timing. I think this is right now! Rahima's only fault in everything that has happened is that she was born too beautiful. I have watched that uncle lusting after her every time I was at a family party. I thought she would be safe at home, but that was not so. To think the father believed his brother over his daughter is a terrible thing. She was a loving and dutiful daughter to him. To think this is the way he treated her!'

Pierre said, 'Your idea is good. Anyone looking for me would not expect a family group. Are you to be my wife Latifa and Rahima our daughter?'

'You would make a very good husband, Doctor. Here many men have young wives, so I think I will be Rahima's mother and your mother-in-law.'

'You will have to stop calling me doctor, Latifa. From now on I will be called by your husband's name, Mustafa. We will wait for three days to let Rahima find her strength again. She is young, so recovery will be fast. She will be sore for a few days, so we must bind her up for her comfort. How do we leave this place, Latifa? I do not even know where we are. I have only seen the hospital since I arrived! I have no idea where we are or what to do, or even what town we are in.'

'We shall go by bus as far as it will take us. I have been saving my money for this. So with you to protect us, we will protect you. After the bus, we may have to walk. I have a map of the city and a map of Syria. I think the best thing is to head for Turkey. What do you think?'

They studied the maps.
'No, I think Lebanon is closer.'
'But there are many refugees already in Lebanon. They have closed their borders. They may not welcome us!'

'I do not plan to be a refugee for long, Latifa. In Lebanon, many of them speak French, which is my language, which will make things easier to negotiate. As soon as I am out of Syria, I intend to go back to France. Do you have a passport, Latifa? And Rahima?'

'Yes, I got the passports as soon as Rahima came to live with me. I knew we would have to leave as soon as the baby was born.'

'I will not leave you stranded, Latifa. Let us give Lebanon a try and we will see what comes.'

They waited for three days for Rahima to recover and set off on the fourth day.

They had no trouble on the way. It seemed the whole population was on the move. There were so many people walking that their story was believed at every checkpoint. Accommodation was not always easy to find, but Latifa's money helped solve that most days. The buses were erratic. No timetables as far as they could make out, but sometimes when they were just about to give up, one would appear to take them in the direction they wanted to go. It took them three weeks to go as far as a car could take them in one day. Pierre knew this was the case but wanted to stay low profile. So far, their disguise was working well for them. Pierre's plan was that as soon as they reached Beirut, they could fly to France.

At last they reached the border of Lebanon and Syria. They did not have visas, so Pierre asked to see the man in charge. A big burly man came over to them and showed the trio into an office. Pierre explained his story, backing it up with his French passport and his medical credentials. He told them of his abduction by ISAS and imprisonment and escape when the hospital was bombed. This seemed not to make an impression on the policeman, Pierre guessed he had heard too many stories to believe any of them now.

Pierre asked if he could make a phone call to Paris. He would pay for the call. The policeman reluctantly allowed it, asking for money upfront. Latifa handed over a handful of change, which the policeman pocketed and then pushed the phone over to Pierre.

He rang Inspector Moreau's private number, which took a long time to answer, but he eventually picked up. 'Who is this ringing me in the middle of the night?'

'Hello, Inspector, this is Pierre Dumont calling from the Lebanese/Syrian border. We are delayed at the border and need clearance to get through to Beirut so that we can fly back to France.'

'You say we? Who else?
Two ladies I have been travelling with, they saved me when the hospital was bombed and I owe them my life. Without them I would be lifeless in a load of rubble which is all that is left of the hospital now.'

''What are their names? I will get them clearance with you. Put me onto the policeman there, and I will see if he can get you clearance on to Beirut.'

After speaking to the policeman for some time, he hung up.
The policeman gave each of them a pass to get through to Beirut, pointing out a bus stop adjacent to the office.

In Beirut at last, Pierre looked for an airline office where he paid for three one-way tickets with his credit card. They would have to stay three days for the flight, so he asked about hotels.

They spent the next three days looking around Beirut. Pierre had been here as a very young man and had loved it. At that time, they called it 'the Paris of the East'. Now he wasn't so sure it lived up to that; he could see huge buildings everywhere, lots of traffic all in a hurry. Lots of apartment buildings housing what could be refugees and was pointed to an area where refugees without any money was housed, a huge compound. He would not like to leave Latifa and Rahima here.

There were some buildings that had been bombed, still with bullet holes in them. So much had changed. He felt sorry for the loss of the old Beirut. It had been a lovely place.

Latifa and Rahima were happy to be going to France. They had not expected it; they thought they would be left behind in Lebanon.

Inspector Moreau met them at the airport. 'We thought you were dead in that bombing of the hospital.'

'I was counting on that', said Pierre. 'They wouldn't come looking for me if they thought I was dead. Latifa saved my life that night.' He went on to tell about the journey they had experienced.

'What do you plan for the ladies now, Pierre?'
'I will take them to my house. Ana will welcome them. They will have to go the usual rigmarole of being accepted as refugees, and I will have to get them permission to stay. I am sure Ana will understand!'

'Ana is in Buenos Aires with the children, staying with her brother and his family. We advised her to go for her own safety. We were upset how the terrorists hoodwinked us. How did they get you out of France?'

'By car to Brussels and then by air to Syria. I was drugged most of the time and didn't come to until we were at the hospital. I was kept prisoner, locked up at night, until Latifa rescued me quite accidentally, the night of the bombing. The bombing was dreadful. If I had been in the hospital that night, I would be dead for sure. It was fortuitous that it allowed us to get away. I think the good Lord has more things for me to do!'

'Will you now go to Buenos Aires?'
'I will get Latifa and Rahima settled first. I owe them a great deal.'
'Do you want me to notify your wife?'

'Yes. Tell her I will be there in a week or so. Then she will expect me and not have heart attack when I pop in.'

'I will drop you all at your house. Do you still have the keys?'
'Yes, my captors never took anything away from me. They were not expecting me to be going anywhere.'

'Your car is in your garage. They brought it back here when they found it with the keys still in it, abandoned at the kerbside of the clinic. We would like to see you tomorrow at 10 a.m. to debrief you. Is that all right with you?'

'Yes, I will see you then.'

Pierre spent a week familiarising his guests with where to shop and spent some time teaching them French. They had been practising since they started their journey, so Pierre thought they would get by. He was confident they could cope. They did not want to contact the Syrian community in Paris. They said they wanted a clean break.

He booked his ticket to Buenos Aires, not knowing what to expect there. He had not been to any of the Americas before and knew nothing about it, as Ana did not talk about her previous country.

When he arrived in Buenos Aires, he was surprised to see a large modern city. He had presumed, because Ana had not wanted to talk about it, that it would be more primitive. What a pleasant surprise!

He told the driver of the taxi to drive around the city for half an hour so he could get an idea of it before going to Sandro's hotel.

He was pleasantly surprised to find a beautifully laid-out city. The Hotel Aria was not downtown but not far from it.

The driver went into the hotel driveway, and Pierre went into the foyer into the reception area. He admired the decor as he went, thinking. Sandro and Bethany were well placed in their society if they owned this.

He asked the receptionist for Sandro Rodrigos. She spoke on the phone for a moment and Sandro appeared.

'Pierre, what a lovely surprise! We were concerned for you, but I can see it is hard to keep a good man down. Come into my office, and I will ring Ana.'

After trying his phone for a few minutes, he said, 'She must be in her car. Looking at the time, I can see it is time to pick up the children from school. It is not allowed by law to use your phone while driving. I will leave a message for her and she will ring me back soon.

'We bought Ana a small car to pick the children up from school. She is living in our town house at the moment. We were not sure whether to make things permanent or leave everything in abeyance. We are so happy you survived the hospital bomb blast!'

'I think the Syrians now think of me as dead, but I am not convinced that staying in Paris is safe for me. The word may get to them that I am alive, and it may start all over again. They certainly need doctors over there.'

Just then the phone rang. It was Ana returning Sandro's call.
'Ana, Pierre is here with me in my office at the hotel. Do you want to come and pick him up, or shall I drive him to your place?'

'I will come right away. The children are with me, Robert too. Can I leave him with you?'

'Sure you can, Ana. See you soon.'
Sandro left Pierre in his office while Sandro went out to wait for his sister and the children.

She arrived minutes later, and he pointed her to his office.
He ruffled Robert's hair and hugged him and then rang Bethany on his mobile to bring her up to date and say he would bring Robert home later.
After half an hour, Ana and Pierre came out of the office. Ana kissed Sandro and said, 'Come to dinner tomorrow night, please.'

Dinner the next night was basic. Ana had no time to make anything special. After dinner, when the children had gone to bed, they sat with a drink and sat waiting for Pierre to start his story. He began at the abduction and finished at the present.

'Regarding our future, it is all up to Ana. I have proposed moving to another city so that I can continue my work and start a new life. It is impossible for me to stay in Paris now. My policemen friends see me starting a new clinic in another city and carrying out the same work as before. Ana is not yet convinced that she wants to do that. Since walking through part of Syria, I am even more convinced that my work is important to France, and I want to go on with it.'

Sandro said, 'So you are proposing to go back to France and continue as you have been for years, despite the dangers of it? This time in another city?'

'Yes, that is it in a nutshell. Ana does not want to go. I can't blame her really. The last few months have been horrible for her. Not knowing where I was and whether I was alive. I can understand her not wanting to go through all that again. All I can see in my mind's eye is the destruction and the people, and I want to go on with my job. It is for France. I do not want to see a France like Syria, and if I can do anything to avoid it, I want to try.'

'What of your marriage? Does it not mean anything to you?'
'It has meant everything to me, but I am not able to turn my back on my country.'

Sandro turned to Ana. 'And you, Ana?'
She said with tears in her voice, 'He has chosen his work over his family. I will stay in Argentina. I cannot bear the thought of going through all we have been through in the last six months again. I never thought I would say it, but I will not leave now!'

Ana asked Pierre, 'What do we do now?'
'You and the children stay here, and I will go back to France, and after six months if we have not changed our minds, we shall divorce. I will have to sell the house in Paris to pay for my new lodging and clinic, and I will send the remainder to you. I will try to come back periodically to see the children.'

Sandro stood up. 'We must be off. We will ring in the morning to see if you have changed your minds.'

****

On the way home, Bethany said' I find Pierre somewhat secretive. What do you think of him?'

Sandro thought for a few minutes and said 'I agree with that thought, He does not say much really, it is mosly generalities. What I have wondered, is why he has never offered to pay anything of his families expenses. He just ignores the fact that we are supplying accommodation and food for him and his family, and that we have bought Ana a car. It seems as if he does not think of things so common. Perhaps Ana has paid all the household bills from her salary in the past. This makes me wonder where he used his double salary, one from the clinic in which he was in charge, and from the government for his spying abilities, which would have added up to a substantial amount each month.'

177

Bethany concurred 'I have thought about all that as well. Not that I begrudge Ana and the children at all. I think when you said that your parents should have left Ana something, it does not seem as if they even thought about her. It was entirely their loss, she is such a lovely person. Though it must have been very hard for Ana without any support from her family from such a young age. I cannot understand their position at all, to neglect your daughter seems so harsh to me.'

'I agree with that statement whole heartedly' said Sandro emphatically 'It must have cost her many nights wondering what went wrong. It was so unfair to her and she must have missed her family dreadfully. That is why I feel Pierre is treating her badly now as well. She does not deserve this double whammy to her life and I am glad she has decided not to go back to France, it would only cost her more heartache, he seems very detached from the situation, merely stating facts and seeming detached from the situation, not thinking of his family. I cannot understand him at all.'

'I expected something like this to happen. If Pierre had decided to stay in Argentina, it would have been all right. Or, if Ana had not reconnected with Frank, things may have been different. She may have followed Pierre!' said Bethany

'You think there is something between them?'
'Maybe not yet. If Pierre leaves her again, I think she will turn to Frank for comfort. Everyone needs someone to love and Pierre has squandered his marriage for the sake of these other ladies in his life. I do not believe he would have come to his decision to stay in France without them backing him up'

The next morning Ana rang to say they had not changed their minds, Pierre was returning to France alone.   Pierre left on Sunday after spending some time with Tamara and Julian.

He had the long trip back to Paris to contemplate his new future. Perhaps Latifa could help him in the new clinic. Rahima could resume some schooling and be housekeeper for the three of them. The more he thought about it, the more he liked it, and he cheered up enormously. It was not really bad news for him after all. If things worked out as he planned it could be a bright future for him.

Ana had many meetings with her grandmother, discussing her position and asking for advice. She suggested Ana ring Frank and make a date.

Ana rang Bethany and asked if she would have Tamara and Julian for the weekend.

Sandro laughed enormously at Bethany's news and said, 'I always suspected you bewitched me, Bethany, and now I am convinced you are a witch to have predicted this. How clever you are to predict this solution. I love you, my own sweet witch.'